M EMER
35250000222935
89a
Emerson, Kathy Lynn.
Face down upon an herbal

6/98

FACE DOWN
UPON AN HERBAL

Also by Kathy Lynn Emerson

Face Down in the Marrow-Bone Pie

FACE DOWN
UPON AN HERBAL

Kathy Lynn Emerson

St. Martin's Press
New York

FACE DOWN UPON AN HERBAL. Copyright © 1998 by Kathy Lynn Emerson. All rights reserved. Printed in the United States of America. No part of this book may be used or reproduced in any manner whatsoever without written permission except in the case of brief quotations embodied in critical articles or reviews. For information, address St. Martin's Press, 175 Fifth Avenue, New York, N.Y. 10010.

Design by Nancy Resnick

Library of Congress Cataloging-in-Publication Data

Emerson, Kathy Lynn.
    Face down upon an herbal / by Kathy Lynn Emerson. — 1st ed.
      p.   c.m.
    ISBN 0-312-18092-6
    I. Title.
    PS3555.M414F32   1998
    813'.54—dc21   97-35456
                                                           CIP

First Edition: April 1998

10 9 8 7 6 5 4 3 2 1

for Sandy

FACE DOWN
UPON AN HERBAL

1

S tartled by a small sound, Magdalen Harleigh looked up
from the herbal she was studying. Lord Madderly's two
towheaded sons moved with studied stealth among the
trunks and aumbrys that furnished their father's private library. Bent on no good, she'd warrant.

"Good day to you, Edward. Philip." Magdalen hopped off
her four-legged, joined stool, abandoning the treatise on poi-
sonous plants propped open on the armariola's inclined lid.

Edward, who was ten, stopped short. Philip was so close
behind that he barreled into his brother, bumping his nose
hard against the stiffened back of Edward's doublet. The
seven-year-old managed not to cry, but Magdalen could tell
from the tortured workings of his mouth and eyes that it was
a near thing.

"Good day to you, Mistress Harleigh," Edward replied.
"We needs must fetch a book to the schoolroom."

He was lying. Magdalen knew because he refused to meet her steady gaze and was toying nervously with the black braid at the hem of his dark green doublet.

"What book?" she asked.

Over the years of her service to the Madderlys, officially as Lady Madderly's companion and waiting gentlewoman, Magdalen had assumed many of the duties of librarian. She knew precisely where every volume was stored and could name a dozen more on related subjects when asked. If her expertise made her a trifle territorial about Lord Madderly's collection, no one else in the household minded. She was useful to them. Efficient.

"A Latin book," Edward said, but he did not give its title.

Another lie, Magdalen thought. What did he want in truth? Barely conscious of her action, she began to scratch her left forearm beneath the loose-hanging gray wool sleeve.

Edward rushed into speech, turning quickly away from her as he spoke. "We know where it is kept, Mistress Harleigh. You need not trouble yourself to help us find it."

"Indeed?" She found this claim even more suspicious. The boys had never previously shown much enthusiasm for books. Rough games and practical jokes interested them far more.

High, narrow windows filled with expensive clear glass provided light to Lord Madderly's library. Two huge fireplaces heated the large, L-shaped room. Between them, fifty large chests and ten small coffers, many of them of cedar, sat on the tiled floor and on top of sturdy tables. They held one of the largest collections of books in all of England. At present it included folios, quartos, booklets, pamphlets, and broadside ballads. Over eight hundred titles in all. Five languages were represented: Latin, Greek, French, Italian, and English.

Lord Madderly also acquired maps, which were stored in a long wainscot box. His collection of letters from famous men filled the drawers behind doors in two carved oak aumbrys.

Magdalen paused in front of a tapestry showing the allegorical figures of Faith, Hope, and Charity and watched the boys' progress. First they stopped at the Dutch-made trunk, its exterior painted with landscapes and flowers. They looked at it with real longing but knew better than to try to open that one. Lord Madderly had for a time used it as a sort of family bank and it had a Spanish-style double lock, the springs of which filled the whole of its lid.

They likewise passed by the long trunk and the great chest bound with iron, coming at last to a smaller version of the latter. This had been designed as a traveling chest. Made of leather soaked in oil to make it waterproof, it had been reinforced with iron fittings. As Magdalen watched, Edward lifted the top, which was curved so that rainwater would run off, and quickly selected a slim volume from the linen-lined interior.

Only then did he look over his shoulder and realize he was being watched. Bright color flooded into his face, but he seemed determined to brazen it out. "Come, Philip," he said to his brother. "We will go back to the schoolroom now."

Philip flushed even more darkly than his brother. The color extended up into the roots of his pale hair.

"What book have you selected?" Magdalen blocked their escape route and held a hand out for the purloined volume, noticing as she did so that there were flecks of blood under her fingernails. A stinging sensation along her arm told her she'd been digging at the rash again.

Edward clutched the leather-bound volume to his chest and ignored her outstretched hand. She wondered what she would do if he simply turned his back on her and walked away. She had no authority over the boys, but she was entrusted with the care of their father's collection.

"Are you certain you wish to take that particular book?" she asked.

The books in Lord Madderly's library boasted a variety of bindings. Some had only paper or vellum covers. Others were bound in calf, sheepskin, or deerskin. A few had colored Morocco leather, which came in blue, red, and green as well as brown and black, and featured gold stamping and tooling. The volume Edward held was distinctive enough, with gilt on the edges of the pages and a black velvet ribbon holding the dark wine red cover closed, that she could guess which title it was.

"Master Wheelwright recommended that we read it," Edward insisted. His high, piping voice came close to being a whine.

That Magdalen doubted, but the boys' reading material was not her responsibility. The preservation of Lord Madderly's collection was.

"If you wish to read that book, you must do so in this room." She resisted the urge to scratch her itching arm, but a dispirited sigh slipped out before she could stop it.

"Our father is master here," Edward reminded her in haughty tones.

"Aye, and that book is one of the rarest in your father's collection. He'll not be pleased if aught happens to it."

To herself, Magdalen admitted that she did have another reason for her objections. The item in question contained nasty French fabliaux full of carnal coupling, profusely illustrated with woodcuts. 'Twas scarce suitable subject matter for boys so young. Almost as shocking as Lord Madderly's copy of *Aretino's Postures*. The household chaplain would be appalled if he heard Edward and Philip had been exposed to such depravity and Magdalen would no doubt find herself the subject of his next sermon for allowing it.

As she sought inspiration for dealing with this ticklish situation, she suddenly sensed a new presence in the library. A glance toward the entry revealed Niall Ferguson, eighth baron Glenelg, the annoying man who had been Lord Madderly's guest this sennight past.

Scholars arrived at Madderly Castle at regular intervals, invited to study the rare volumes the baron had collected. Sometimes other collectors visited, or booksellers came with stock to sell. Magdalen had been told Lord Glenelg had a deceased relative's book collection to dispose of, but he was taking an extraordinarily long time about completing his business.

Glenelg strode through the library as if he owned it, stopping briefly to stare at the balcony on the second level. That area, about the same size as the musicians' gallery in the great hall, could be reached only by a flight of wooden steps at the southern end of the library. It held storage chests and aumbrys full of material which, while still precious, was used less frequently than the rest of the collection. Lord Madderly's study, the room he'd set aside for private contemplation, was also reached by way of those stairs.

What unpleasantness, Magdalen wondered, was Lord Glenelg plotting? In the short time he'd been in residence at Madderly Castle he had managed to intimidate or alienate almost everyone with whom he'd come in contact.

Mistress Magdalen Harleigh was no exception. She did not care for Lord Glenelg. She was made wary by a hint of cruelty in his piggy little eyes. His air of superiority set her teeth on edge.

Besides that, two days past, she had caught Lord Glenelg snooping among the private papers she kept here in the armariola. He'd insisted he was only looking for the small, fat, parchment-bound book in which she recorded new acquisitions, and he'd surrendered to her the sheets of foolscap he'd been holding clutched in one beefy hand, but she did not believe his disclaimer. She only hoped he'd not had time to read what she'd written.

The distraction provided by Glenelg's progress through the library gave Edward the chance to bolt. Magdalen just managed to catch him by the collar.

"Not so fast. The book, if you please."

"Why should they not have that book?" Lord Glenelg asked in his raspy, irritating voice. He came near enough for Magdalen to smell the noxious scent he used in a futile attempt to mask foul body odor. Something with civet, a musky aroma she could not like no matter how expensive it was.

Obviously enjoying the fact that he made her uncomfortable, Glenelg smoothed the fabric at the front of his plum-colored doublet over a considerable paunch and regarded the two boys solemnly. After a moment, he held out one hand.

To Magdalen's disgust, Edward immediately relinquished his treasure. Glenelg opened the volume, flipped through a few pages, then handed it back. His lips quirked, exaggerating sagging jowls in a fleshy face. His small dark eyes glinted with malice.

"Off with you, lads," he said. "Who is Mistress Harleigh to refuse? Why, she is naught but an upper-level servant, your stepmother's companion, whatever that implies."

The younger boy shuffled his feet, glancing warily in Magdalen's direction. Edward accepted the windfall and made a hasty exit, leaving his brother to follow. After an indecisive instant and an even more wary glance at Glenelg, Philip did so.

Magdalen heaved a long-suffering sigh, one that started on a high note and ended with the expulsion of air an octave lower. Then she deliberately drew herself up to her full height, relishing Lord Glenelg's frown of displeasure. Knowing she was his social inferior did not quite quell his annoyance at being forcibly reminded she was taller than he.

Gratified at scoring a point, even if she had lost the match, Magdalen prepared to resume her work, but Lord Glenelg was not finished with her. His pudgy fingers snatched up the herbal she'd left on the armariola.

"What is this?" he demanded. He answered his own question by reading the title aloud. *"A Cautionary Herbal, being a compendium of plants harmful to the health."*

Glenelg let the book fall open at random and silently perused the page. His face purpled at what he read there, forcing Magdalen to hide a smile.

The treatise, written by an anonymous herbalist who used only the initials S.A. for identification, described the effects of various poisons. Its stated purpose was to warn against the accidental ingestion of dangerous herbs in foods, simples, and compounds, but in effect it actually gave recipes for many deadly combinations. A useful sort of guidebook, she thought, if one wished to rid one's self of an annoyance.

Lady Madderly had recently told Magdalen that this anonymous author was a woman, the wife of a courtier. The S. stood for Susanna; the A. for Appleton. Magdalen thought she might like to meet Lady Appleton one day. It was not impossible. Lady Madderly was already corresponding with her, for Lady Madderly was working on an herbal of her own.

"You tried to confiscate that book from the boys," Glenelg said. " 'Tis only just that this one be kept out of your hands." He tucked it inside the front of his doublet, through an opening at the waist.

Magdalen did not trouble to point out to him that the boys had gotten away with their prize. Although it was an effort to hold her tongue, she did not protest his high-handed behavior, either. Nor did she lose her temper.

"No doubt you will find it fascinating reading," she told him. She had other work she could do. From the open shelves of a nearby livery cupboard she removed the copy of *Liber de arte distillandi,* a volume she'd earlier extracted from a chest of such books.

Patience, she cautioned herself as she began to take notes for Lady Madderly. Glenelg would not dare keep the herbal long, not if he wished a successful conclusion to his business with Lord Madderly. She could wait to read it. She would not give this infuriating man the satisfaction of quarreling with him.

As if bored by such an easy victory, Glenelg returned to his contemplation of the balcony. He'd just started toward the stairs when he was interrupted by the arrival of Beatrice Madderly, his host's sister.

Magdalen felt a moment's envy when she noticed how splendidly the other woman was dressed. Beatrice could afford the best and indulged herself, though at times her sense of what went well together was somewhat lacking. She favored pale shades like maiden's blush and sheep's color and they had the unhappy effect of making what was normally a pale complexion even more pallid. This day, however, she was wearing one of her most flattering gowns, a creation of lion-tawny velvet. It was lined with orange-tawny taffeta, edged with black velvet and trimmed with black cony. Just the sight of all that sumptuousness made Magdalen feel drab and unimportant in her ash-color kirtle.

"My dear lady!" Glenelg turned his full attention to the noblewoman.

At the sight of the Scots lord bearing down on her, Beatrice's expression froze. Magdalen suspected she was fighting an urge to spit in his eye, but instead she squared her shoulders and forced herself to smile. He was a guest here. She was his hostess. Courtesy was required.

After a moment, at Glenelg's whispered urging, she accompanied him to one of a series of windows set into the thick outer wall of the library. Unlike the higher openings, these were filled with colored, patterned glass. Curtains of yellow say hung at the sides of each recess, behind facing seats cushioned with embroidered pillows. Glenelg sat down opposite his victim, keeping one hand on her arm, and continued to speak in low tones.

Watching them, Magdalen told herself she should be grateful Beatrice had distracted him. Glenelg was the noblewoman's problem now, not Magdalen's.

She fiddled with the plain falling band at her throat, smoothing the strip of linen between her thumb and forefinger. One hand fell to the embroidered forepart that showed through the inverted V of her kirtle and she touched one of the flowers done in silks of murrey, russet, and whey. Magdalen knew she was foolish to feel envy, but there it was. She did covet the other woman's position. Were Lord Madderly Magdalen's brother—

She cut off that thought before it had fully formed. She had no cause to complain. She'd done well for herself at Madderly Castle. She'd do even better once Glenelg was out of the way.

Magdalen went back to her note-taking with a new sense of dedication, but from time to time she stole glances at the couple in the window embrasure. At first they seemed to get on well enough, but before long they appeared to be openly quarreling. Magdalen did not imagine anyone could long endure Lord Glenelg's superior attitude, not even Beatrice. From the look on her face, she longed to strike him.

Sympathizing with the impulse, Magdalen once more bent over her book. She studiously avoided looking toward the couple at the window but could not entirely ignore them. She could hear the rise and fall of their voices and discern a note of agitation in Beatrice's tone even though she could not make out any of the words they exchanged.

Whatever their debate, it came to an abrupt end when the daylight began to wane and a servant arrived to perform the late afternoon ritual of lowering the candle beams and lighting the tapers. By the time he raised the iron supports to the ceiling again with the aid of a pulley, Magdalen had gathered her papers together and placed them inside the desk and was returning her book to its proper place.

She did not realize Lord Glenelg had abandoned Beatrice Madderly until he appeared at her elbow. The lid of the book chest closed with more force than she'd intended.

"The key, Mistress Harleigh."

"Key, Lord Glenelg?" She blinked at him in confusion.

"To Lord Madderly's study. His sister tells me you have it and I wish to study certain books he keeps there."

Magdalen looked around for Beatrice, who had blatantly lied to Lord Glenelg on the subject of this key, but the other woman was nowhere in sight. Magdalen suspected she'd ducked around the corner made by the room's L shape and left by way of a secret door hidden behind a huge panel of arraswork, abandoning Magdalen to deal with Lord Glenelg.

"I am sorry, my lord, but Lord Madderly is most particular about his study." She tried to sound polite but firm. "It is his rule that no one enter that room unless he is there to issue an invitation."

He rarely extended one. Lord Madderly would not even let the maids in to straighten and his wife had been specifically banned from the premises.

Glenelg's lips curved into the threatening glimmer of a smile. At the same time he drew from its black leather sheath a small sharp dagger with an ornately carved handle. Magdalen's sharp eyes picked out a crest with a bee and a thistle.

Ostentatiously, Glenelg began to clean his fingernails with the blade. "Ah, rules. Foolish rules," he murmured.

"Foolish it may be, but Lord Madderly is master here and must be obeyed."

A derisive snort answered her. To emphasize his contempt, Glenelg used the knife to gesture toward the balcony. "Rules are meant to be broken." The blade swung threateningly close to the tip of Magdalen's nose. "You, my dear young woman, will hand over your key or I will tell Lord Madderly what I found among your papers."

Magdalen's hand flew forward in a vain attempt to knock the knife aside, but Glenelg was too quick for her. Laughing unpleasantly, he returned the blade to its sheath, turned his back, and started toward the stairs.

"Come with me, Mistress Harleigh," he commanded.

"But I do not have a key," she protested as she scurried along in his wake. She wondered how far he was prepared to go to get into that room. She was shaken by his threat to reveal her secret, but also concerned that he might break the lock and enter if he was left to his own devices. She'd not put such behavior past him.

A masculine voice interrupted their progress. "May I assist you, Lord Glenelg?"

Magdalen was unsure whether to feel relief or embarrassment. Master Wheelwright, the schoolmaster, lean as a whippet and quiet as the pet ferret he kept, had slipped into the library without either of them noticing.

"Will you return this to its proper place?" Wheelwright asked, his voice full of sympathy as he held out the book his charges had made off with earlier. "I do not imagine you intended the young masters to abscond with it."

"My thanks," she murmured. "I will do so at once."

So saying, she turned her back on the two men. As she

did, a flash of tawny and black caught her eye. Beatrice Madderly. She had not left the library, but stood hidden behind a tall aumbry. When Magdalen stared at her, she held a finger to her lips. Clearly the noblewoman intended to stay where she was and eavesdrop.

Magdalen pointedly went about her own business. Even so, as she replaced the volume in its book chest, she could not help but be aware that Master Wheelwright and Lord Glenelg were engaged in an intense conversation. Beatrice wore a frown, likely because she was unable to overhear any more than Magdalen could.

And none of this, Magdalen reminded herself, was any of her business. Taking the opportunity to escape, she whipped behind the arras and darted out through the small door it concealed.

2

Lord Glenelg was once again cleaning his fingernails with his elaborate little bye-knife when the person he'd been waiting for appeared on the balcony just outside Lord Madderly's study.

"You have kept me waiting," Glenelg complained.

"So I have." There was a certain pleasure in thwarting this offensive Scots nobleman, a heady excitement in the danger of it.

"You were warned." Glenelg bristled like an affronted hedgehog, but he still seemed to think he had the situation under control, that he was in command.

He was wrong.

"Warned or not, there is no help for it. I've no intention of letting you enter this room."

"You will regret your rashness."

"What do you think lies inside, that you are so determined to see?"

"More proof of your guilt, mayhap." Glenelg's annoying chuckle was as counterfeit as a passport bought for twopence at a fair. There was no true mirth in his soul. If he even had a soul.

"I think you wish to gain entry for the sheer perverse pleasure you get from knowing and doing what others do not."

Glenelg did not like this insubordination. His small eyes glittered with animosity. "You will do as I say or I will see to it that all your wicked deceptions are revealed to the world."

"By doing so, you would implicate yourself."

"I will be long gone ere my part in this business comes out. You alone will suffer. Do you know what they do to traitors? 'Tis a horrible death." For emphasis, Glenelg gestured with his knife as he described in loving detail the torment of being hung, then cut down alive to be drawn and quartered. "A quick death is far better," he concluded.

"Then you shall have one."

Glenelg looked surprised when his blade was knocked away, plucked up, and thrust back at him, piercing his heart as it plunged through plum-colored velvet and into his chest.

He crashed back against the door to the study and was bounced forward by the impact. The book he'd had tucked into the waist of his doublet fell free, landing with a thump on the wooden floor. A moment later, Glenelg lay sprawled on top of it.

The killer left him there. Face down upon an herbal, the dead man awaited discovery by whatever person next entered Lord Madderly's library.

3

Minstrels played in the gallery of the great hall as Gilbert Russell, Lord Madderly's gentleman usher, performed his ceremonial duties before supper. He marched in through the screens at the back carrying a thin white rod as his badge of office and proceeded to the lord's table where the family and all important visitors were seated.

They were served according to their rank. It was Gilbert's responsibility to set this order and to make sure there were enough servants in Lord Madderly's gray livery, the baron's arms embroidered on each long, loose hanging sleeve, to wait upon the entire company assembled for the meal.

Just ahead of Gilbert marched a yeoman carrying a torch. To Gilbert's mind this was a useless holdover from the past, since the hall was well lit with candelabra. Above their heads hung a huge bronze chandelier of Flemish make. No less than nine branches held fat candles and at the very top of the ornate piece there perched a kneeling angel.

Behind Gilbert in the processional came a servant carrying the great salt, a heavily decorated silver container which he set before Lord Madderly's place at table. More servants brought platters and dishes, placing some on the serving table just inside the hall and bringing others directly to the dais. The table there was a solid, permanent piece of furniture resting on six sturdy carved legs held steady by low-set stretchers.

"Give place, my masters," Gilbert called out, even though no one blocked his path. That, too, was ceremonial, the traditional command for the meal to begin.

The chaplain prayed only briefly, since Lord Madderly preferred not to delay the pleasures of the table.

Gilbert would not eat until much later. For now he had the responsibility of making sure all went smoothly. If more bread was needed, it was Gilbert who notified the pantler; if beer ran low, he told the butler to bring more.

In the background the musicians played taborette, lute, and rebec in a lively tune, but neither that nor the constant clatter of cutlery and plate were sufficiently loud to prevent Gilbert from monitoring the conversations at several tables at once. Lord Glenelg's empty place next to Lord Madderly was soon remarked upon. That the Madderlys troubled with this formal meal at all was in his honor, or rather because it was better thus than supping with him in more intimate surroundings.

"It is not like him to be late," Lord Madderly said. "Never have I seen such a valiant trencherman."

"Ill, do you think?" his sister, Beatrice, asked.

Eleanor, Lady Madderly, short, square, and overweight, her ample proportions emphasized by the bright jewel tones she preferred, gave Beatrice a smug smile. "The more for us," she said.

Henry, third baron Madderly, also bordered on the obese. He toyed with his bucknade, pushing the thumb-sized gobbets of meat aside to pick raisins and almonds out of the cinnamon and sugar sauce. Was he concerned about Glenelg? Gilbert doubted it. The Scot had worn out his welcome days ago, but Lord Madderly had his own reasons for encouraging this particular guest to stay longer.

"Mayhap he is sulking," Beatrice suggested. "The poor man did seem frustrated by his unsuccessful attempt to gain access to your study."

"What? My study?"

"Yes, Henry." Beatrice spoke to him as if he were a child, but in fact she was several years younger than he. She was a handsome woman in a horse-faced, hawk-nosed way, and even Gilbert had to admire her magnificent bosom.

"By Saint Anthony's Fire!" Madderly exclaimed. "What business did he think he had there?"

"None he would own to, which is why I would not fetch the key for him when he asked for it."

"Man's a great disappointment," Madderly grumbled. "I have yet to see the books he claimed he had to sell."

"The fellow is malevolent," Lady Madderly said.

"Aye. The very word."

Below the dais, servants were seated and served in accordance with both their master's rank and their own. From the first of these tables, where Lord Madderly's household officers and Lady Madderly's companion sat, Gilbert heard the same fabric of conversation picked up and embroidered upon.

"He asked me for that key, too," Mistress Harleigh confided in her husband.

Gilbert studied her with a critical eye. The woman was too tall for his taste. Emaciated in body, though she ate well enough. Her complexion was sallow, her cheeks hollow, and her nose long and thin as a blade. Then there were her annoying habits. She sighed. Deeply. Loudly. Frequently. And she scratched when she was agitated. Apparently she was agitated this evening. One hand had completely disappeared beneath her sleeve. It emerged to seize upon a tiny portion of moorcock pie.

Otto Harleigh, Lord Madderly's master of horse, paid no mind to his wife, preoccupied with a grilled slice of mutton stuffed with shredded onions, egg yolk, parsley, spices, and suet.

"He also asked me about procuring Lord Madderly's key," Master Wheelwright offered. The schoolmaster reached for the boiled beef, then began to feed the choicest bits to the red-eyed, pale-furred ferret draped over his shoulder. Gilbert failed to see the appeal of keeping such a creature as a pet. If it bit one more servingman, he vowed, he would ban it from the great hall during meals.

Gilbert scanned the other tables. All seemed to be going smoothly. Servants trudged back and forth between the tables, every step on the rush-covered floor releasing the faint scents of the rosemary and lavender leaves strewn there along with the fleabane.

On the dais, however, Lord Madderly still was not eating with his accustomed dedication. He seemed to be quarreling quietly with his wife when he felt Gilbert's gaze upon him. First he glared at him, then beckoned for his gentleman usher to come forward.

"Go you and look for Lord Glenelg," he ordered. "It is not like the man to miss a meal. Look first in his chamber, and question his servant. Then go you to my study, to be sure the fellow has not found some way to get in."

Reluctantly, Gilbert went, tucking the rod into the placket at the front of his doublet. There it was kept at all times when he was not carrying it, one end sticking out in order that strangers to the household should at once know his position. More bother than honor, he'd decided after the first week, but there was no help for it. Two months past, he'd agreed to perform the duties of Madderly's gentleman usher until all was resolved. He was resigned to do so as diligently as he could.

It was dark in the library when Gilbert entered. The tapers in the candle beams had burned down and gone out. Without sight, other senses grew more acute. Gilbert knew the faint smell that greeted him. He ordered Peadar, Lord Glenelg's serving man, to fetch torches, then fumbled for the tinderbox and candles customarily kept on the small table just inside the door.

The cavernous room loomed before him, made eerie by shadows. There were geometrical patterns and animal and bird motifs in the plaster above his head, but not enough illumination to make them out. With only the single taper in the latten candlestick for light, Gilbert could barely discern that there was a ceiling.

But he could still smell death, together with the distinctive odor of civet. He knew what he would encounter when he followed his nose, climbing the stairs to the balcony. It was as well he'd been the one sent to find Lord Glenelg, Gilbert decided. He'd not like to think of one of the women stumbling over the body.

For a moment he just stared down at the remains, fighting an absurd urge to chant, as they did for kings, "Lord Glenelg is Dead. Long Live Lord Glenelg."

Instead he knelt next to the body and turned it over. The handle of Glenelg's own knife still protruded from the wound that had killed him. By the light of his candle, Gilbert recognized the Ferguson family crest, something he had not noticed on the previous occasion on which he'd seen Glenelg's bye-knife. His reaction was immediate. He removed the murder weapon from the corpse.

There was no spurt of blood. Glenelg's heart had long since stopped pumping it through his veins. Gilbert cleaned the blade on the dead man's doublet, then secreted the knife on his own person, next to his wand of office. No one must see that crest.

Was there anything else on Glenelg's person that might implicate someone in his murder? Well aware he did not have much time before Peadar returned, Gilbert quickly searched the dead man's clothing. He found nothing of significance. Later, he decided, he would examine Glenelg's possessions. For the moment he turned his attention to the book.

The body had fallen atop a small, leather-bound volume. Gilbert picked it up and leafed through it, but it was only an herbal and he did not find anything between its covers that related to Glenelg's presence at Madderly Castle. He dropped it back where he had found it and turned to survey the scene around him, holding the candle high. Nothing incriminating leapt out at him.

At the sound of approaching footsteps, Gilbert glanced once more at Lord Glenelg and frowned. Even in death, the man complicated Gilbert's life.

Circumstances seemed to dictate that he now give every appearance of searching for the killer, but he'd need to tread warily. The authorities would look no further than Gilbert himself if they ever learned of his connection to the dead Scotsman.

4

Upon his arrival at Leigh Abbey, Sir Robert Appleton's country house, Walter Pendennis insisted he be shown directly into Lady Appleton's presence. "She is in her stillroom, sir," the housekeeper said.

"Then take me there."

He thought he knew what to expect. He had known Robert since they were young men together and although he had never met Lady Appleton, Pendennis had heard a great deal about her.

Some of it had been unflattering. Robert most often complained about her intelligence. She'd been educated like a man by a doting father, which in Robert's opinion had spoiled her for true womanliness.

"She'll not be pleased to be interrupted," the housekeeper warned. A woman of middling height who appeared to be about to give birth, she addressed him with an asperity that was anything but servile.

"I fear I must insist. I bring a message from the queen."

Relenting, though she did still seem annoyed, the woman escorted him to a large stone building separate from the house. "Wait here," she instructed and left him cooling his heels in the herb garden while she went in alone. Before he had time to do more than glance at his surroundings, she was back, her expression sullen. "Go in if you must, but do not interfere with Lady Appleton's work."

Pendennis had been under the impression that activity in the stillroom reached its peak during the summer months, when most herbs were prepared for storage. Then he remembered. Lady Appleton experimented with powders and decoctions. Her preoccupation with poisons kept her busy year-round.

He sniffed cautiously as he ducked to miss the low lintel of the door and was rewarded with a pungent combination of odors. He had an excellent nose, but these aromas were at first too well mingled for him to sort out any single one.

A tall, slender young woman met him just inside the door. This was not Lady Appleton, but from her uncanny likeness to Sir Robert, Pendennis could guess her identity. One night, late, at Queen Elizabeth's court, when Robert had been deep in his cups and brooding, he'd confessed more than was his wont. He'd confided that he had a half sister, a girl whose existence he'd not even suspected until that business in Lancashire two years ago.

"You are Catherine," Pendennis said.

"Aye, sir. Catherine Denholm." As he moved past her,

deeper into the stillroom, he caught the scent of violets. The housekeeper came in after him, closing the door behind her and leaning back against it. Fascinated by Catherine, Pendennis dismissed the servant from his thoughts.

"My name is Walter Pendennis."

"Sir Robert's friend." She smiled, charming him.

"Aye."

If Robert did not want to acknowledge the relationship, Pendennis thought, he'd best keep Catherine close in the country. To any who had ever met Robert Appleton, the resemblance would be impossible to miss. Catherine shared with her half brother a narrow face, a high forehead, and distinctively dark brown eyes. The most likely assumption would be that she was his bastard daughter. By Pendennis's reckoning, Catherine was just sixteen.

"I am sorry to interrupt your work," he said, "but I have been sent by Her Majesty the queen."

The woman standing at the long wooden table at the center of the room glanced his way. When their eyes met, he was startled by the intensity of her gaze. Her eyes were blue, most ordinary in color and shape, and yet Pendennis was suddenly certain that this was a woman who missed nothing. Apparently confident that his presence did not signify distressing tidings about her spouse, she gave a curt nod in acknowledgment of his arrival and went back to her work.

"Lady Appleton will be free to speak with you in a moment," Catherine said. There was no note of apology in her voice. She was simply stating a fact.

The hands busy with mortar and pestle, grinding some sort of dried root to powder, were strong and work-hardened and stained with the residue of various herbal preparations. Delicate, lily-white fingers such as those seen at the royal court had no place here.

"No beauty," Robert had said of his wife. 'Twas true. She was tall for a woman, square-jawed and sturdily built. And yet she had an aura of competence about her that was attractive in itself. Pendennis, an avid student of architecture, had learned to appreciate both form and function.

"Master Pendennis." Catherine's lilting voice interrupted his thoughts. "May I have your assistance?"

She handed him a down pillow, the casing open at one end, and as soon as she was sure he had a good grip on the edges she began to stuff in crushed and dried leaves and flowers from each of several containers.

Sniffing cautiously, he identified two. "Violets," he said. "Your favorite, I do think. And chamomile."

The girl's smile was sweet and shy. "Aye. And hops, balm, and mullein. These herbs, replaced every few weeks, encourage peaceful sleep."

Pendennis held more pillows, a task which allowed him to study his surroundings at the same time. Robert's wife was now mixing the powder she had made into a stiff paste. When she was satisfied with its consistency, she rolled it out on a board as if it were bread dough. After considerable kneading and pounding, she began to pinch off small bits and form them into tiny balls with her hands. It was then Pendennis realized she was making pills.

On the table where Lady Appleton worked sat all manner of equipment for distillation—alembic, pelican, matrass—as well as empty jars, pots, and other vessels made of stoneware, ceramic, glass, horn, pewter, and iron. From force of habit,

Pendennis began to assess the contents of the stillroom. He counted thirty large containers, labeled and dated, and over a hundred smaller vessels. Some had parchment tied over the mouths while the covers on others were made of thin skin.

Drying herbs hung in bunches from the beams above his head, but what, he wondered, was kept in that black chest in the darkest corner of the room? Phials of poison? He had reason to think that might be so.

Lady Appleton startled him by speaking his name.

Pendennis saw that the pills were all shaped and had been left to dry on the board. Lady Appleton wiped her hands on her apron and tucked an unruly strand of dark brown hair back up under her embroidered cap.

"This is an unexpected pleasure, Master Pendennis," she said. "Your pardon, sir, for my rudeness in ignoring you, but even a short delay in the preparation can spoil the result."

"It is I must beg your pardon, madam, for disturbing you, but I have come with a message from the queen."

"So you said, but if you hope to find my husband here, I fear your journey was in vain. He has been gone since before Michaelmas. By now he should be in Scotland."

Pendennis had to hide a smile. He well knew where Robert was, and something of what his old friend had been obliged to deal with during the last few weeks.

"My message is for you, Lady Appleton. Queen Elizabeth would have a favor of you."

Many a woman would have been flustered by that announcement. Not Lady Appleton. Pendennis supposed he should not be surprised, given what he'd heard of her.

"Damnably self-assured," Robert had once called her. The description fit.

Susanna Appleton's first impression of Walter Pendennis was that he had a typical courtier's face—bland except for the eyes. It amused her to note that he had grown his beard in the style favored by Lord Robin Dudley, the queen's acknowledged favorite. Susanna recognized it because her husband had done the same.

A pity, she thought now, that the effect was so unflattering. The Dudley style consisted of a mustache that drooped down on each side to the corners of the mouth, a tuft of hair beneath the lower lip, and below that a short chin beard.

Pendennis was a bit taller than Susanna, with a figure that suggested he liked beer, ale, and French wines a bit too well, though she thought perhaps 'twas muscle yet, not fat. She could see little of the structure of his arms beneath the heavy sleeves of his buff-colored doublet, but the legs beneath the padded, pleated skirt looked strong and well-shaped. This was amply revealed by the current form-fitting fashion in thigh-high leather riding boots. Her gaze flicked to his padded and decorated codpiece with only cursory interest before her attention was captured by what he was saying.

"The queen wants you to pay a visit to Madderly Castle."

"Why?" She had recently been in correspondence with Lady Madderly, who was engaged in compiling an account of every plant found in England, including their properties, virtues, and descriptions.

"Lady Madderly is writing an herbal, but she progresses slowly," Pendennis said. "It is Her Majesty's desire that the author of *A Cautionary Herbal* go thither to assist her lady-ship in the preparation of this great work. The queen believes Eleanor Madderly's book will be definitive, a godsend to wives and apothecaries alike. It could become a fixture in every household, second only to the Bible in importance."

"And how," Susanna asked, "does Lady Madderly feel about having me thrust upon her?"

She studied Pendennis's eyes as she waited for his answer. He had an intelligent look to him and there had been kindness in his gaze when he'd helped Catherine with the pillows, but she could not help being suspicious.

What had Robert told her about this man? That he was lazy. That he collected the most useless bits of information, which on occasion were surprisingly helpful. And that he was a sometime intelligence gatherer for the queen, as well as a courtier and diplomat, as was Robert himself.

"Lady Madderly welcomes your assistance," Pendennis assured her.

Susanna had her doubts, but one did not argue with a royal command. For all Pendennis's pretty phrasing, she understood that she was obliged to accept this assignment. It would reflect ill on Robert if she refused.

A glance at her companions revealed that Catherine seemed intrigued by the conversation. Jennet, once Susanna's tiring maid, long her friend and companion, and now her housekeeper, affected boredom but was in fact hanging on every word.

"When does the queen wish me to arrive at Madderly Castle?" she asked Pendennis. "It is in Gloucestershire, which is some distance from Kent." Lady Madderly had indicated it was near the border with Warwickshire, in the Cotswold Hills. Susanna knew little of the region save that the sheep raised there were popularly known as Cotswold lions.

"The sooner you can begin, the better," Pendennis answered. "The best route to take is by way of London and Oxford. From Oxford the road runs north to Burford, then west and north toward Campden, some thirty miles beyond."

Campden, Susanna recalled, was the nearest market town to Madderly Castle. "How long am I expected to stay?"

"Until the herbal is ready for publication."

She hid a grimace. 'Twas plain he had no inkling of how much work was involved. Lady Madderly even meant to include woodcuts to illustrate the plants. It was an ambitious project, one which might well take years to complete. "You ask me to abandon my household on a moment's notice and for an indefinite period of time."

"You will be amply compensated."

Susanna knew all about the queen's idea of compensation. She expected her courtiers to spend their own money in her service and rarely rewarded them with material goods or property. Even when she lavished a peerage on one of her subjects, it was likely to come without a sufficient source of income to support the title.

Susanna was about to suggest that they go into the house, there to take refreshment while she discussed the matter with Catherine and Jennet, when Catherine spoke.

"You must accept, Susanna," she said. "The queen expects no less."

"To go at once means I'll not be present when Jennet needs me." The younger woman was due to give birth in less than two weeks. A midwife was already in residence.

32

Jennet herself gave a snort of wry laughter at that. "This child, like the last, cares little who is present at the birth. Go you to Gloucestershire. Never mind about me."

Susanna fought a smile. She knew Jennet well. Even in childbed she'd enjoy being the center of attention. And since her husband was the newly appointed steward here at Leigh Abbey, having successfully filled that post at another Appleton property for nearly two years, she would be treated as well as any gentlewoman of the household when her time came.

"I do not like to leave you," Susanna protested. "Indeed, I do wish I could take you along."

That was clearly impossible, but Susanna had the feeling she'd have need of a friend at Madderly Castle. Something in Pendennis's manner suggested he was not telling her everything about this mission.

That suspicion, however, was not enough to make her refuse the queen's request. It was not every day that a woman's scholarship and expertise on a subject were recognized, let alone sought out. In a way she was flattered. Master John Day of London had printed her book at the end of the previous year, but anonymously. Few people knew she was the S.A. who had painstakingly compiled it.

"If you mean to go, go. You should be glad of something to do in the winter, since it is such a slow season. 'Twill be especially dull with Sir Robert gone."

"Could I come with you, Susanna?" Catherine seemed taken with the idea.

Perhaps it was time for the girl to explore a wider circle of friends, Susanna thought. This seemed a painless way to achieve that end. "Are there any objections to my bringing a companion, Master Pendennis?"

"You may bring an entire retinue if you wish."

She lifted an eyebrow at that. He was much too eager for her to agree, confirming her suspicion that there was more going on at Madderly Castle than he had revealed. No matter, she decided. She would deal with whatever else awaited her there when she arrived. The sooner the better, as Pendennis had said.

"Very well, Master Pendennis," she said. "Catherine and I will be ready to leave in two days' time."

5

The red-haired, green-eyed Scotswoman giggled. Sir Robert Appleton smiled.

His facial muscles felt stiff, unaccustomed to the expression. Hardly surprising. He'd had few occasions to feel either amusement or pleasure since he'd been sent to this benighted land on his queen's behalf.

"Ma belle," he chided her, "you tempt me from my duties. I am here to wait upon the Queen of Scots." Mary, widow of Francis II of France, was sovereign of Scotland in her own right. Like Elizabeth of England, here a woman held power over male subjects. 'Twas a perversion of the natural order, or so Sir Robert believed, but he was careful never to express that traitorous thought aloud.

"She will not see you today." Annabel spoke English badly, as did her royal mistress. "She has already ridden away."

"Without you?" They were seated close together in one of

35

the small, private window embrasures at Holyrood Palace, shielded from prying eyes by the curve of the thick stone wall. He dared to press the palm of his hand to her stomacher.

"I told her I had a . . ."—she struggled for the English word—"ache of the head."

"Speak in French," he advised. The queen and her ladies were fluent in that language, and in Inglis, the barbaric tongue of the lowland Scots. Some had Latin, as well.

Robert did not know whether to be flattered or annoyed by Annabel's ploy. He'd hoped to speak with Queen Mary today, to convince her that her cousin Elizabeth had only Mary's best interests at heart when she proposed Mary give up any claim to be heir to England's throne.

"Where has her royal highness gone?" he asked.

"To hunt, and taken all her retinue with her save for me." Annabel giggled again. "She wishes to show off the French horses you helped recover. And the new saddles we had made. All of us have new riding cloaks, too, but they are black, for mourning." She sighed. "I will be glad when the year for King Francis has passed. I do so like bright colors."

Robert made the flattering remarks his mistress expected of him, but his thoughts had returned to those damned horses. Was it his fault one had died? Queen Mary seemed to think so.

Thirty royal horses had been shipped from Dieppe when the young queen left France. She'd landed safely at Leith, two miles distant from Edinburgh on the Firth of Forth, in an early-morning fog on the nineteenth day of August. The horses she'd counted on having for her grand entrance into

Edinburgh after a thirteen-year absence had made landfall on English soil and been detained there.

Held for ransom, some would say.

Sir Robert Appleton had been sent north to handle the delicate negotiations for their return. He considered that he'd been spectacularly successful. On the sixteenth of October, the twenty-nine surviving steeds had been released into the hands of thirty Scots sent south to fetch them and ride them the sixty miles from their prison in northern Northumberland to Edinburgh. Two days later both they and Sir Robert had arrived safely.

Had he received any thanks? No. Instead he'd faced the Queen of Scots's anger because one of her precious mounts had died during its captivity. She did not care that injuries during the earlier sea voyage had caused the animal's death. She wanted restitution, and ever since that first day she'd been looking at Sir Robert's own stallion, Vanguard, with greedy eyes.

"Robert?" Annabel's sultry voice brought his wandering attention back to her. She boldly took his hand from her stomacher, where it had been inscribing lazy circles, and moved it up to cup one soft breast. Abruptly, Robert decided he was glad he'd missed the queen. What better way to pass an afternoon than to dally with a French-bred Scotswoman with inventive tastes?

"Come to my lodgings," he urged her.

"But then 'twill be an hour or more before we can truly be together."

"But here we have no privacy," he reminded her.

He also thought the interior of Holyrood Palace a dismal

place. Its thick walls and deep-set windows covered with iron gratings made even the queen's apartments close and gloomy. Annabel's tiny chamber, shared with others of the queen's lesser ladies-in-waiting, lay deep within a rabbit warren of passages and rooms.

"I will leave and you may follow soon after," he said.

"Cowgate Port has an impertinent guard," Annabel complained. "I like it not when I must explain myself."

"Then do not come in disguise, *ma belle*." She'd worn the garments of a merchant's wife the last time she'd visited him in Edinburgh. "A visor will serve to hide your identity and yet all will know by the richness of your dress that you are a person of importance, not to be trifled with."

"Why could you not live in Canongate, outside the boundaries of the city? 'Tis so much closer."

" 'Tis safer within the wall." And the Cowgate section of Edinburgh, for all that it had such a bucolic name, was the area which contained the residences of many noble families of Scotland, as well as those of several city councilors. The location suited him.

Annabel sulked. She teased. She kissed and caressed. In the end, she unlaced his codpiece, lifted her skirts, and had her wicked way with him right there on the window seat.

The experience was unique and altogether enjoyable while it lasted, but by the time Sir Robert rode back out of Holyrood Palace, across the iron drawbridge and up the long, broad street paved with great square stones, he was appalled by the risk he had taken.

He came into the suburb of Canongate, full of solidly built, close-packed houses, almost immediately after leaving the palace. Within a half mile he reached the heavily defended gate at Netherbow Port, centered between the two royal properties of Holyrood Palace and Edinburgh Castle. Annabel was right. The guards at all the gates asked impertinent questions.

Once through the great central tower of Netherbow, Robert's gaze was drawn up High Street, a wide paved road that ran along the spine of a ridge to the castle some four and a half furlongs to the west. Tall wooden tenements crowded close to it along the rock upon which it perched. He looked away almost immediately, refusing to be impressed.

Closer to hand were the other landmarks of the city. Very close at hand, since all of Edinburgh enclosed only 140 acres within its walls. He was already approaching the Mercat Cross. Just beyond, midway between Netherbow gate and the castle, stood St. Giles's Collegiate Church, crowned with stone in the shape of a lantern tower decorated with fretted pinnacles. From the pulpit within, John Knox ministered to his flock, preaching sermons against the rule of women.

Robert thought Knox was a fool to speak so openly.

He did not ride past the church, or the old tolbooth in front of it or the newly built tolbooth and gaol just beyond. Instead he turned his horse south. The ridge sloped steeply away on both sides of High Street and he quickly found himself moving downhill through narrow closes and past tall, close-packed timber-framed houses. Cowgate, between the old city wall and the new, had lately been a wealthy suburb. Robert's lodgings were on the upper floor of a tall, stately dwelling built of local squared stone. It boasted its own stable and upon dismounting he handed Vanguard's reins to Fulke, the groom he'd brought with him from England.

Tugging on his forelock, Fulke shuffled his feet, indicating he had something to say. "A messenger waits for you inside, sir," he finally blurted. "From the queen."

Fulke was a strapping, rough-skinned fellow, but his cheeks were red with the embarrassment of having to speak to one of his betters. He was more comfortable with only the horses for company.

"Our queen or the Scots queen?"

"Queen Elizabeth, Sir Robert."

"Who has come?" Sir Robert asked. "Did you recognize him?"

Fulke shook his head and looked more ill at ease than before. The feeling communicated itself to Sir Robert. These were dangerous times. Was a legitimate courier from the English queen within, or had his lodgings been infiltrated by some enemy sworn to kill him?

"How do you know this man came from the queen?" he asked Fulke.

The servant brightened. "I did see the privy seal, sir. On some papers he had."

Sir Robert doubted Fulke would know the queen's privy seal from any other, but his wariness eased a trifle. At least Fulke had known enough not to let a stranger into the house without seeing some form of identification.

One hand resting lightly on the dagger he wore at his belt, Sir Robert climbed the stairs to the first floor and opened the door to the solar. The Scots housekeeper he'd hired came bustling up behind him, carrying a tray piled high with cakes and ale. He let her enter first.

"Ah! Sustenance!"

At the sound of that familiar voice, Robert relaxed completely. "Pendennis," he said. "Welcome."

"You may not think so after you learn why the queen sent me."

"I'll not give up Vanguard," Robert warned.

"No one has asked you to." Pendennis made free with the contents of the overflowing tray.

"Queen Mary makes her desires very plain without saying a word."

"I passed the royal entourage on my way here. 'Twas a veritable pageant. Sixteen beautiful young women, the queen herself but a fresh-faced girl of eighteen—"

"Fifteen young women," Robert corrected him.

"Fifteen, then," Pendennis said agreeably. "I did not attempt to count the number of gentlemen, messengers, pages, maids, equerries, masters of hawks and hounds, and armed outriders who accompanied them, though I did notice they had more than a dozen bulging hampers of food. And the horses. I could scarce help mark them, for they did make a splendid sight."

"The queen, in spite of still being in mourning, dearly delights in showing off both her horses and herself."

"And are those horses still the talk of Edinburgh?"

"Interest waned when some were sent to Stichell to be bred at the royal horse farm."

"From what I could see, they are fabulous beasts, far superior to the nags Scots are accustomed to ride."

"You have not come here to talk of horses. What did bring you to Scotland?" Robert helped himself to ale, noting with displeasure that it was cloudy, a sign it was newly brewed. He sipped, grimaced, and reached for a seedcake, but only a few crumbs were left on the tray. "Have you had sufficient? I'd not want you to starve."

Pendennis ignored the sarcasm and contentedly patted his stomach. " 'Twas a long, hard ride to reach here."

Robert did not doubt it. If Pendennis had come from London with a message from the queen, he'd have ridden post horses all the way, changing his mount every thirty miles. One could cover up to one hundred and fifty miles a day, but that pace was killing.

"Three days on the road?" he asked.

"Four," Pendennis said, "but I started from Leigh Abbey."

Robert paused in the act of lifting his tin-glazed earthenware tankard to his lips. Leigh Abbey? His own home in Kent? "What business had you there?"

Unperturbed by the sharp note in his friend's voice, Pendennis calmly explained. "I was sent to your lady wife by the queen. Lady Appleton and Mistress Denholm should arrive at Madderly Castle within another day or two."

"Madderly?" He'd met Lord Madderly once, years ago, but knew little about the man except that he did not often visit the royal court. "Why?"

"She has been asked to assist Lady Madderly in the preparation of an herbal."

"The queen sent her there for that purpose?"

"Aye. And to give you an excuse to spend Christmas in Gloucestershire."

"I do not follow your logic, Pendennis." He was not certain he wanted to.

"There has been a murder at Madderly. Lord Glenelg. A Scot."

Robert did not know the name. "What's that to do with me? Or with my wife?"

Pendennis refilled his own tankard with ale before he answered. "The queen is concerned because Glenelg may have been part of a treasonous conspiracy at the time of his death."

"And Susanna is to find out if he was?"

Pendennis looked startled. "Nay. She knows naught of the queen's suspicions. Her instructions are to help Lady Madderly. The queen thought of her because it was the cautionary herbal Lady Appleton compiled which was found under Lord Glenelg's body. And because Lady Madderly and her ladies are working on a great herbal they hope to see published."

"What was the herbal doing beneath a corpse?"

"The murder took place in Lord Madderly's library." Pendennis paused, taking a long swallow of his ale. "Landing on that book was no doubt mere coincidence, but it put the queen in mind of you and your lady wife, and that is to the good. She looks to you to learn the truth in this matter of treason and to find Glenelg's killer. There's doubtless great honor in it for you if you succeed."

If. There was the rub.

"What is known of this conspiracy?"

"Passing little. Glenelg is believed to have gone to Madderly Castle to meet a master forger. There have been recent reports of counterfeit passports and bills of exchange emanating from the Cotswold Hills. You will appreciate that with relations between Scotland and England as shaky as they are, a Scots nobleman's death, whether he was involved in treason or not, must be handled with the greatest diplomacy."

It was not just relations between Scotland and England that were shaky. They were at sixes and sevens within Scotland. And within England, too, now that Robert thought about it.

"Susanna should have been told the truth. She'll likely ferret it out for herself, and then there will be hell to pay for keeping secrets from her."

"That was my impression as well," Pendennis admitted. "I felt . . . uneasy lying to Lady Appleton. Your wife, Robert, is a daunting woman. I was most astonished by her efficiency. I've met few females who could pack and be ready to leave home so quickly."

That Robert could well believe. Susanna delighted in organizing things, including other people's lives.

"So, I am to visit Susanna at Madderly Castle at Yuletide." That gave him two or three weeks yet before he'd need to leave Edinburgh. "Have I any more than what you have already told me to go on? Is there some person already suspected of Glenelg's murder?"

"No one. We know only that he was stabbed through the heart and that the weapon was removed from the scene of the crime. Glenelg's own knife was also missing. Logic dictates they were one and the same."

"I like this not," Robert muttered.

Treason. Murder. Subterfuge. But most of all, Sir Robert Appleton did not like the fact that the queen had decided to involve his wife.

6

MADDERLY CASTLE

W ell, Catherine," Susanna asked, "what think you of this Madderly Castle?" They had arrived in late afternoon and pled exhaustion following supper to retire to the inner chamber and withdrawing room assigned to them in one of four great square towers.

"It is very large. And luxurious." She indicated the bed she and Susanna were to share. It was furnished with feather beds, down pillows, fine linen sheets, thick woolen blankets, a quilt of Spanish felt, a tapestry coverlet, and hangings of sea green Genoa velvet to contrast with the gilded wood.

Her mentor and friend smiled as she, too, studied the room's contents. No amenity was lacking, Catherine thought. Two wainscot stools were padded with velvet cushions. There was a press in which to hang clothes, with shelves for caps and gloves. There was even an oblong carpet on the waxed and polished oak floor. It had to be at least four ells long and two ells broad. Catherine had seen carpets before, but they were so expensive that most people used them to cover tables rather than risk the wear caused by walking on them.

The arrival of the tiring maid assigned to them curtailed conversation and Catherine suddenly realized she was going to have to be careful what she said while she was at Madderly Castle. She was accustomed to a small household, since only eighteen persons made up the entire staff at Leigh Abbey. Here there had to be well over a hundred servants.

Except to tell them her name was Nan, the maidservant said not a word, but under Susanna's supervision she unpacked the capcases. The contents took up little space in the press and there were naught but two combs to go on the table beneath the looking glass and keep company with a tall, fat candle, capable of burning for a full hour, and a slender glass vase containing dried flowers.

"Our trunks will arrive by common carrier sometime in the next few days," Susanna told the servant girl. She did not trouble to explain that they'd brought only the small traveling bags with them in order that they might make their journey on horseback.

Each mounted on sidesaddles on their own palfreys, Catherine and Susanna had ridden from Kent to Gloucestershire with an escort consisting of four burly menservants, also mounted. This had enabled them to complete their journey, with the judicious use of ferries and barges to speed them along, in just five days.

When Nan had everything in order and had helped both Susanna and Catherine strip down to linen smocks and woolen stockings, she stoked the fire and left them till morning. She would sleep on a pallet in the outer room, to be ready to serve them again whenever either of them called her name.

"She is very quiet," Catherine observed.

"A change from our Jennet," Susanna agreed. She drew the hangings back and climbed up onto the bed, curling her legs beneath her. "Now that we are private together, I would have your impressions of this place and its people."

Catherine frowned. "If you wish to learn of the lesser servants, I cannot help you. They ate in the great hall. The table I shared in the parlor contained only the household officers and Lady Madderly's companion."

Susanna lifted her eyebrows at Catherine's tone of voice. "You sound as if you resent being excluded from the company in the great chamber."

"I am a considerable heiress. If the Madderlys knew my true relationship to Sir Robert, that I am his sister and a knight's daughter, would I not have been asked to sup with the family as you were?"

Instantly she felt ashamed of herself. Susanna and Robert had been very good to her. She knew full well they might have left her in the keeping of cousins in Manchester and ignored the inconvenient fact that Sir Robert's father had also sired Catherine.

"Your pardon, ma'am," she said before Susanna could respond. Bobbing in an exaggerated curtsey, she tried to make light of her complaint. "I am your companion, am I not, madam? May I not help you roll down your stockings?"

Susanna slapped at the hand reaching for the brightly colored fabric. They were both wearing stockings they'd dyed themselves. Susanna's were a shocking yellow, produced by the use of weld. Catherine's had been treated with woad and come out a brilliant blue.

"You know you are a great deal more than that, Catherine. And feeling sorry for yourself is not an admirable trait. Besides, you doubtless had the more enjoyable meal. Lady Madderly did naught but complain of her husband's two sons. She is his second wife and she thinks they resent her."

"And Lord Madderly?"

"He is a man intent upon his own concerns. He took little notice of his wife and less of me. In truth, he was so lost in thought that he very nearly dipped his bodkin beard in the rice pottage."

Picturing it clearly, Catherine was unable to contain a giggle. Lord Madderly's graying beard grew from the center of the chin, so long and pointed that he must be at almost constant risk of catching it on things. But she was not ready yet to abandon her complaint.

"Rice, is it? None of that expensive imported delicacy reached the parlor."

"Next you will tell me you were forced to eat the fumosities."

With a sniff of disdain, Catherine pretended to be horrified by the thought. "No such insult was offered. The carver knew better than to serve up such inferior parts of fish, flesh, or fowl, though no doubt the *lower* servants had to make do with the legs and chops and heads."

A grin answered her. "This from a girl who delights in a nice dish of Garbage."

"Only when it is made with giblets," Catherine protested.

She did love those, chopped fine and stewed, then thickened and spiced with mace and pepper.

"Take your complaints about the food to Beatrice, Lord Madderly's sister. If you dare." An exaggerated shudder underscored Susanna's feelings toward that lady.

"What is so terrible about Beatrice Madderly?"

"She is frighteningly efficient. Since both Lord and Lady Madderly have scholarly matters to occupy their time, neither troubles to oversee the upkeep and provisioning of the castle. It falls to Beatrice to ensure that the place remains vermin-free and that there is plenty to eat."

From Susanna's wry tone and from the fact that she ran Leigh Abbey with like efficiency, Catherine deduced that this was not the real reason she had developed an aversion to Beatrice.

"I am not certain what to think of the woman," Susanna continued. "All through the meal, when she thought I would not notice, she cast resentful glances in my direction. Did your supper companions say anything to you that would explain Beatrice's reaction to my arrival?"

"Mistress Harleigh had naught but praise for you," Catherine assured her. "She confided to me that she and Lady Madderly are the only ones who know you are 'S.A.' and then she said, in a whisper, that she thinks a woman's writings should be acknowledged. She ventured the opinion that you should have insisted that your name appear on *A Cautionary Herbal.*"

The fire in the hearth had begun to smoke fitfully. Catherine crossed the room to poke at it just as a downdraft stirred the coals. Coughing, she made her way to a window and flung it open wide. It was too dark to see much outside, even though a bright crescent moon was rising.

"Lady Madderly mentioned in a letter that Mistress Harleigh has been a great help to her in writing the herbal."

"Her husband, Otto Harleigh, was also at table with us. He is master of horse here."

"The tall, gangly fellow with the round beard like a rubbing brush?"

"Aye. His talk is all of horses and hers is all of herbs. I do wonder what they find in common when they are alone together."

When Susanna did not reply, Catherine glanced her way, then winced at her own insensitivity. She might have been describing the Appletons. Was Susanna thinking of Robert? Did that account for the peculiar look on her face?

"Have you encountered the man with the pickedevant?" Catherine asked more to get them off the subject of mismatched husbands and wives than because she wanted to discuss him. The short, pointed chin beard and curled mustache made the style distinctive.

"I have not had that pleasure," Susanna said.

"He is the schoolmaster. John Wheelwright by name. He has a most interesting pet. A ferret. It rides about on his shoulder and eats off his trencher."

"I have heard that some people keep ferrets. I cannot say the idea appeals to me. I saw a ferret kill a cat once, which did not endear me to the species."

"This one seems friendly, though I was not seated close enough to Master Wheelwright to tell for certain. The chaplain and the steward were between us."

"Had you conversation with any but Mistress Harleigh?"

Susanna asked. She had climbed under the covers and now leaned back against the pillows. Her eyes were already drifting closed.

Catherine, on the other hand, felt not at all sleepy. The crisp cold air coming in through the open window had revived her. "No more than to be asked to pass the cheese," she answered. "The steward, Master Borden, who has a very fine swallow's tail beard, and the chaplain were deep in their own quiet conversation, which seemed to center on the advisability of letting beer age at least a month before drinking it. What we were given to drink was brewed but eight days ago."

"I had a brief glimpse of the chaplain," Susanna said. "He muttered prayers before the meal and then fled, no doubt anxious for his own food." She paused, then added with a small chuckle, "He was clean-shaven."

Catherine smiled. "Aye." He was also quite bald. She had not heard anyone mention his name.

"Between us we seem to have met everyone of importance," Susanna said. "It remains to be seen how we will deal with them in the weeks to come."

As they'd talked, Catherine's eyes had become accustomed to the darkness beyond her window. Their room overlooked the ribbon of road that led to the gatehouse, which was set between this tower and the one to their north. A single horseman was just leaving the castle. Catherine leaned out. Even from this height and distance, she recognized his long, lean lines.

Gilbert Russell. The one other person of whom she had taken note while she supped. A tiny sound of feminine appreciation escaped her, for he was a most handsome man.

"Catherine? Did you say something?"

"What did you think of Master Russell?" she asked. Reluctantly, she turned from the window and faced the bed.

"The name means nothing to me."

"The gentleman usher," Catherine clarified, painfully aware that what answer her friend and mentor gave was important, much more so than she'd anticipated when she posed the question.

From Susanna's frown, Catherine judged she was having difficulty calling up any impression of a man carrying a wand of office.

"He is young for the post," Catherine said helpfully. "His hair is cut short and was all but concealed by his bonnet, but I do think it is likely to be more red than brown."

"And his beard?" The smile in Susanna's voice triggered a nervous giggle on Catherine's part.

" 'Tis decidedly more red than brown."

"Neat and close-cropped," Susanna said. "I remember him now. I could scarce help but notice that short ceremonial gown. Brocade it was, in gold, black, and crimson, and lined in crimson, too, and sporting a large collar of white fur. For some reason I also remember his shoes. They were made of velvet and decorated with small slashes. Master Russell has been provided with most fine livery."

"He is a most fine gentleman," Catherine murmured.

How could Susanna not remark upon his eyes, which were an unusual color of blue, like the sky on a perfect summer's day?

"Never tell me you are smitten!" Susanna was teasing, but Catherine considered her words most seriously.

"You have always said it was inevitable that at some point I would succumb to the disease of love."

"I had been praying you'd prove immune." She regarded Catherine somberly for a moment. "Let us hope it is but an infatuation and will pass. He is not for you," she added bluntly.

Catherine did not argue. Instead she fell silent and went back to staring out at the moonlit landscape.

The rider had passed out of sight. She wondered where he had gone, for it was passing strange that anyone, even a big strong man like Gilbert Russell, should choose to ride out alone at night.

7

First thing the next morning, Catherine at her side, Susanna broke her fast on bread and ale and then accompanied Eleanor Madderly to her husband's library. Beatrice Madderly and Magdalen Harleigh were waiting for them there and they spent a happy hour examining chests and boxes full of books.

"My husband prefers that only a few volumes at a time be taken from this room," Eleanor explained, "so some of our work is done here and some in the stillroom and the rest in my own private workroom in the northeast tower."

"Have you divided the labor among you in some way?" Susanna asked. It seemed only reasonable that they would have, but all three women looked surprised by the suggestion.

" 'Twill go much more quickly if you do so," she pointed out. "And now that there are five of us to share the burden, the tasks may be accomplished even faster." Too late, she wondered if she could have been more subtle in pushing for changes in the way things had been done. She did not want to have to deal with hurt feelings and bruised pride. On the other hand, she had tacitly agreed to stay until the work was done and she had no desire to remain indefinitely at Madderly Castle.

"Does Mistress Denholm share your affinity for herbs?" Eleanor asked.

"I propose she handle clerical duties," Susanna said, deliberately sidestepping the question. Catherine's natural aptitude lay with animals, not plants. Horses. Dogs. Cats. And now, it seemed, ferrets.

"She might be more use in the schoolroom." Beatrice did not bother to hide her dislike of any change. She was obliged to tolerate an acknowledged herbalist like Lady Appleton, but she saw no reason why she should have to put up with Catherine's presence.

In a mild tone of voice, Susanna repeated her suggestion. "Catherine can spare us much labor by undertaking the duties of a scribe. She is meticulous and unfailingly accurate." She was also a keen observer with an eye for detail. Susanna had learned to value Catherine's impressions of people. Here at Madderly Castle, she suspected she'd need any insights she could get.

Eleanor gave her sister-by-marriage a sharp look. "We will allow Catherine to work with us, at least for the present."

All four women turned toward the girl, only to find her staring at the balcony above. "What is kept there?" she asked.

Magdalen blanched. Eleanor blushed. Beatrice's stone-faced expression hardened further.

Eleanor was the first to recover her composure. "My husband's private study lies above, and a small storage area of no great importance."

Into the little silence that followed her statement came a sigh so deep it seemed to make the air shimmer around them. Magdalen Harleigh had made the remarkable sound. Now she was looking pointedly at the other two women, clearly willing them to speak.

Beatrice sniffed disdainfully.

Eleanor frowned.

Magdalen began to scratch industriously at the back of her hand. Blood welled up in the tracks of her fingernails, but she didn't seem to notice. "You have a right to know, Lady Appleton," she said. "A man was murdered up there just over four weeks ago."

Startled by the news, Susanna did not immediately speak, but her lack of verbal response signified neither sudden fear nor any sense of revulsion. She sent Catherine a warning glance, in case her young friend was about to blurt out more than Susanna wished known of the events in their mutual past, then fixed a questioning gaze on her hostess.

"Eleanor, I do think you must provide more details of this distressing event. Has the murderer been caught?"

"We have no idea who killed Lord Glenelg or why."

"Glenelg? I do not know the name. Who was he?"

"A Scots baron."

Susanna exchanged another look with Catherine. A Scot, when Sir Robert Appleton was currently in Scotland on the queen's business? She did not believe in coincidences.

"You did not know Lord Glenelg?" Lady Madderly asked.

"I've never even heard the name ere now. Why did you think I might have?"

"Because when he was found, he was lying face down upon an herbal. Your herbal, Lady Appleton. The one you compiled."

Susanna felt her own face blanch. "My book?" Her hands clenched into tight fists at her sides as she fought the urge to say more. With a shake of her head, she fell silent, but anger was building beneath that calm surface.

She had been deceived when she was asked to come here. Perhaps she could assist Lady Madderly with her herbal, but 'twas clear now that there had been more to the request than that.

Nothing irritated Susanna more than being manipulated.

"I would hear more of this Lord Glenelg," she said when she had a grip on her temper.

"He was a nasty, offensive man," Magdalen Harleigh told her.

"He was stabbed through the heart," Beatrice said.

Eleanor Madderly said nothing, but she had a considering frown on her deeply lined and fleshy face.

"Was Lord Glenelg interested in herbals?" Susanna asked.

"He was interested in making life miserable for everyone around him," Magdalen said. "He came into this room that day just as I was attempting to keep Edward and Philip, Lord Madderly's sons, from walking off with a book they had no business reading. He aided and abetted their mischief and then plucked up the herbal, which I had been reading, and carried it away with him. No doubt it simply fell out of the front of his doublet when he was stabbed."

"A pity it was not so positioned as to stop the blade," Susanna mused.

To her surprise, none of her companions echoed the sentiment. No one appeared to mourn Lord Glenelg's passing.

"He caused a good deal of inconvenience by being murdered," Beatrice complained. "The coroner had to be called. The local justice of the peace made inquiries, disrupting the household. And after all that, no one was arrested."

That, Susanna suspected, must have been the most disconcerting development of all. Resolved, when time permitted, to inquire further into the matter, she allowed Lady Madderly to turn their conversation to herbs and herbals.

8

Gilbert Russell was not certain what to make of Catherine Denholm. She had been at Madderly Castle only three days, but during each of them she'd managed to place herself directly in his path.

On the one hand, he was flattered. She was an attractive lass, especially with all that long, thick, dark brown hair hanging loose beneath a silk caul. On the other hand, that outward sign that she was a maiden made him wary. She was of gentle birth and old enough to marry. Dalliance was unwise unless he wished to run the risk of becoming a husband.

Still, her chatter was entertaining. He knew more than he wanted to know about her childhood home near Manchester and about Leigh Abbey, where she'd lived with Lady Appleton for the last two years. He believed he'd received accounts of every cat, dog, squirrel, and rabbit she had ever rescued.

"What do you think of Master Wheelwright's ferret?" he asked her.

There was a long pause. "His name is Bede. I tried to befriend him, but he bit me."

He couldn't contain a chuckle. "A nasty beast."

"Oh, you cannot blame the poor animal," Catherine objected. "He does not know any better. No doubt he believed I meant him some harm."

"You are too generous, Mistress Denholm." Naive as well as young. Ten years his junior, at the least. Some would say that was the ideal span between husband and wife, but Gilbert had always thought to take a bride close to his own years.

Bride? Where had that thought come from? He was not interested in marriage. Not now. That being the case, a wise man would stay as far away from Mistress Catherine Denholm as he could.

Gilbert knew himself to be clever. He made no claim to be wise.

"Let me see the injury," he said. "There is danger of infection if you do not tend to such bites."

Obligingly she held out her hand. "I know that well, sir. Lady Appleton is well versed in the healing properties of plants and most insistent that everyone under her roof take care with injuries and illnesses."

He took her fingers in his and carefully examined each one, enjoying the feel of her soft skin and the smell of the violet-scented perfume she wore. The bite was small and already healing, but he lifted her hand to his lips and kissed it anyway.

"Master Russell!" she protested, blushing prettily.

Her reaction made him want to kiss her again, this time on the lips, but he fought down the impulse by reminding himself that he ought to be questioning the girl, not making love to her.

He did not know why Lady Madderly had sent for Lady Appleton so soon after the murder, but he had to wonder if there was some connection, especially since he'd twice overheard Lady Appleton asking questions about Glenelg and his untimely death. Her interest came from more than idle curiosity. He was certain of that, though he could not say what it was that convinced him.

"What did Lady Appleton recommend to heal this grievous wound?" he asked.

"She washed it with water of self-heal and then applied a paste made of Saracen's root, and to be safe she had me drink an herb water made of chamomile, dittany, scabious, and pennyroyal, to counteract any poisons that might have gotten into my blood." She stifled a giggle. "She said ferrets qualify as venomous beasts."

He could not help but smile back at her. "Doubtless she will contribute much to Lady Madderly's herbal."

"Indeed she will. And 'tis most generous of her to come here, too. She has already had published an herbal of her own making, and so has no need to do more to make her reputation."

Gilbert gave her a sharp look. A book? An herbal? Could it be?

" 'Tis a very useful volume, too," Catherine continued in a voice filled with pride, "all about dangerous herbs one should learn to avoid. 'Tis called *A Cautionary Herbal.*"

Well, Gilbert thought. There was the connection he'd been seeking between Lady Appleton and Lord Glenelg.

He just wished he knew what it meant.

9

odykins." Lady Appleton cursed under her breath and
regarded the closed door with growing irritation.

Where were all the servants when she needed one?
Although she ordinarily preferred to fend for herself and
found the presence of so many liveried retainers a disconcerting nuisance, just now her arms were overflowing with
material she'd collected from Lord Madderly's library and
the heavy oak door to Lady Madderly's tower workroom,
which she'd taken particular care to leave open, had been
locked against her.

Where on earth had Eleanor Madderly disappeared to?
She'd been hard at work on a new translation an hour earlier.
Susanna considered the possibilities. Her hostess was devoted to scholarly endeavors. Was she still within, intent upon
some task? Had she closed the door to ensure greater privacy?

"Eleanor?" Susanna called out. And called again, at greater volume, but received no answer.

In frustration, she kicked one of the oak door panels. The effort yielded no better result than her shouting and did considerable damage to her toes.

In the shadowy reaches of the passageway that led to the northwest tower, Susanna thought she saw movement. Relieved, she turned for a closer look, ready to call out and request assistance, but when she stared directly at the spot she saw no one. A rat, she decided, and shivered in spite of her warm camlet gown.

Balancing manuscript pages, a copy of *The Secrets of Alexis*, that recently published collection of cures for diseases, wounds, and accidents, and a goblet still half full of the mulled wine Magdalen Harleigh had pressed upon her against the winter's chill, Susanna fumbled for the key she expected to find tucked into the pouch hidden in a placket in her kirtle. The tepid liquid sloshed, threatening the safety of the remainder of her burden. Several pages detached themselves from the manuscript and fluttered to the stone-flagged floor.

Susanna struggled to control her impatience. With exaggerated care, she stacked the papers into a neat pile at her feet, used the book to weigh them down, and went to collect the strays. Before she made another try for her key, she drained the last of the wine from the goblet. There was no sense in risking an accidental spill.

Her second foray into the deep placket produced a bit of lace torn from a cuff earlier that day and not yet replaced, a needle and some thread, which she'd intended to use to , make those repairs, her flint and steel for lighting candles, a broken quill, and several scraps of paper with notes scrawled upon them. The elaborate brass key she was seeking was not there.

"Bodykins," she muttered again.

She'd left the key inside the locked room, on the writing table Eleanor Madderly had assigned her.

With no other alternative, Susanna began to retrace her steps, then stopped. The stairs she'd just climbed went up to the leads and down to the chapel and thence into the courtyard, which she'd just crossed from Lord Madderly's library. On the level just below her, however, was the schoolroom, from which raucous sounds had been issuing when she passed by. She had no desire to encounter those two young hellions, Lord Madderly's sons.

It would be preferable to follow the passageway on this level until she could descend into the kitchen wing. There the steward had his business room and, with any luck, a duplicate key she might borrow until she'd reclaimed her own.

The route led along a raised walk. She'd been told it had once led to a fortified prison tower on the north side of Madderly Castle, but had been modernized by Lord Madderly's father, the second baron. Enlarged window openings had turned it into a long, wide gallery that overlooked the Gloucestershire countryside on the one hand and the former bailey, now transformed into a courtyard with an ornamental garden, on the other.

On the opposite side of the garden she could see the new wing, rebuilt of Cotswold stone by the first baron. Madderly bragged that his grandfather had surmounted these rooms set against the fourteenth-century curtain wall with twisted brick chimneys in order to proclaim that comfort and luxury would be found within.

Anxious to get another key, return, and resume her work, Susanna hurried along. She encountered no other living creature, not even a rat, over the entire distance from tower to tower. She did not expect to run into anyone at the top of the winding stair that descended within that second tower. It was a decided shock when she all but collided with Gilbert Russell.

Even to someone of Susanna's height, Gilbert Russell was tall. He caught her easily before she could bowl him over and send both of them tumbling down the stone steps.

"Are you always in such a rush, Lady Appleton?" he inquired as he set her back on the landing. One brow lifted as he asked the question and that, taken together with his tone of voice, was most provoking.

"You have no call to be impertinent, Master Russell."

He grinned at her, showing large, surprisingly even teeth.

Susanna's eyes narrowed and she regarded him with sudden suspicion. Gilbert Russell was Madderly's gentleman usher, but he seemed to have few duties other than at mealtimes. This was not the first occasion on which he had popped up in an odd location with no apparent reason for being there.

As she studied him, he watched her with a cool, almost contemptuous detachment. She had been quite right to tell Catherine to avoid him, Susanna decided. The man was a throwback to the days of King Henry, when all men cared about was wenching and fighting.

"It is impolite to stare," she told him.

"I do but admire your beauty."

She did not believe that for a moment. Robert was wont to call her handsome, but that was the best that could be said for her physical attributes.

"If you think compliments will color my opinion of you, you are much mistaken, sirrah." She chose the word deliberately. *Sir* would grant him status as her equal and though he obviously thought he was, she begged to differ.

"Your pardon, Lady Appleton." He sketched a mocking bow, briefly doffing his black velvet hat. The high, stiff crown was a wonder in vertical pleats and he'd decorated it with a jeweled broach holding an aigrette. "How may I serve you, then? You seem in a perilous hurry to get somewhere."

"I require a key to Lady Madderly's workroom." Her words sounded more imperious than she'd intended. Wry self-mockery nearly brought a smile to her face. Self-defense. Gilbert Russell made her uneasily aware that she was female.

How Robert would laugh, she thought, to see her so discomfited by this puppy.

"Wait here," the puppy said. "I know where the extra keys are kept."

As she watched him descend the winding stair in rapid, graceful bounds, she acknowledged the real reason he affected her so strongly. He reminded her of her absent husband, both in form and content. She did smile then. Like Robert, Gilbert Russell had a courtier's arrogant swagger. Self-confident, Robert called it. Pompous, overweening pride, she was wont to counter. She wanted better than that for Catherine.

Still, though Susanna hated to admit it, she did occasionally miss her overbearing husband. She wondered how he was faring in Scotland, dealing with the queen's frivolous cousin Mary. He had a difficult assignment this time. She did not envy him practicing diplomacy at a court rife with religious turmoil, political plots, and, if the rumors were to be believed, romantic intrigue as well.

According to Master Pendennis, Robert had already succeeded in the first part of his mission. He would doubtless prevail in the task remaining, whatever it might be. For a moment, Susanna wished she had gone with him. She'd not have been in his way. She'd likely have been of some assistance.

But he had not requested her company and she had not asked to go. And had she accompanied him, she'd not have been at home to receive the queen's request to assist Lady Madderly in her great work. Her suspicion that there was more to her presence here than an expertise with herbs was as strong as ever, but although this was her fourth full day in residence, she had no more idea what she was expected to accomplish than she had when she'd arrived. Surely if the queen had wished her to investigate a murder, Walter Pendennis would have said so.

She'd been asking a few subtle questions anyway. Natural curiosity drove her to that, even though she knew she'd do better to concentrate on the herbal. She could no more stop wanting to know who had killed Lord Glenelg than she could cease wondering about the much more minor mystery this day had brought.

Where had Eleanor gotten to? Susanna peered through the nearest window. There were only three routes the lady of Madderly could have taken out of her tower. This passage was one. The stairs provided two more. If she'd gone up instead of down, she might have left the tower and walked along the leads from the top level of the tower, but Susanna could think of no reason why Eleanor would have done so. It was cold out there, and windy, too.

"Lady Appleton?"

She whirled around, startled to find Gilbert Russell had not only returned but was standing directly behind her. The man crept on cat feet!

"Have you the key?"

"Aye, I have a duplicate here, but you must tell me, Lady Appleton, what became of your own."

"Not that it is any of your business, but I left it in the workroom and in my absence Lady Madderly locked the door."

His brows knit together in a puzzled frown. "She has left the tower?"

"I do presume so, since she did not respond to my knocking." Impatient to return to work, Susanna snatched the key he held loosely between two fingers.

She captured it, but with equal ease he captured her, placing one hand on the wall behind her head to prevent her escape. "Are all educated females so disinclined to engage in conversation?" he asked.

"Call you this . . . conversation?"

His lips twitched, as if he fought a smile.

In spite of her annoyance, Susanna found herself softening a little. The fellow was a rogue, a charming knave like her Robert. And, also like Robert, he apparently could not resist a challenge. She was quite sure he had no interest in her as a woman. He was younger than she by several years and handsome enough to attract not just Catherine, but every other marriageable female at Madderly Castle. This was merely a ploy to force her to acknowledge his superior, masculine presence.

"I perceive that you are one of those ignorant lads who reckons all females should be silent and obedient and lacking in intelligence," she said.

"And passing beautiful, as well."

"Then you've no reason to dally here with me, Master Russell. Get you gone."

"You wound me deeply, Lady Appleton."

"And you, sirrah, condemn yourself to a dull wife if you seek beauty before wit. I do much pity you." She gave him a hard shove, freeing herself, and strode rapidly away in the direction of the other tower.

His good-natured laughter followed her.

Susanna resolutely dismissed him from her thoughts, determined to concentrate on the task at hand. She would need to, for prior experience had taught her that it required both hands to unlock the door to the tower workroom. First she twisted the key a half turn to the right, then a quarter turn to the left while at the same time rattling the latch. On her second try she was rewarded by the sound of a loud click.

As she gave the oaken portal a push inward, she stooped to retrieve the materials she'd left on the floor. Out of the corner of one eye she caught sight of Lady Madderly's green velvet skirt. The baroness had been there all along, sitting at her writing table just inside the door, too immersed in her own endeavors to notice anyone else.

"Really, Eleanor. There was no need to lock me out." Susanna scooped the books and papers into her arms and, still crouching, tilted her head to look up and in.

From that awkward stance, she watched the opening

grow wider. Her view of what waited for her inside expanded.

She went abruptly still. The manuscript pages slid unnoticed from suddenly nerveless fingers and slithered to the floor. The book of cures tumbled after them.

Susanna straightened, then took one cautious step forward. This could not be real. Was it possible she was hallucinating? The idea that someone had drugged her wine was more palatable to her than the sight before her.

Eleanor had not heard her calling. In truth, Lady Madderly would never hear anyone voice her name aloud again. She lay sprawled forward, her head and shoulders resting awkwardly atop herbals, sheets of foolscap, empty cups, and dirty dishes—the usual litter that covered her writing table. Her eyes were open, her face frozen in a surprised stare that seemed to be directed at the heavy silver candlestick lying on the table a few inches in front of her nose.

There was blood on its base, and on the papers and books, and seeping out from beneath the bottom edge of Lady Madderly's close-fitting linen coif, which had been knocked askew by the blow that killed her.

Susanna did not scream. Her stomach twisted once as bile rose in her throat, but she fought down the nausea.

Step by slow step she made a wide circle around the dead woman and reached the smaller table just beyond, the table where her own work lay waiting.

Though she had no doubt at all that Eleanor was dead, Susanna touched her hand. Startled, she jerked back. The fingers were still warm. When Susanna disturbed them, they loosed their hold on an object that tumbled to the tiled floor with a clatter.

For a moment Susanna could neither breathe nor think.

Panic assaulted her in waves as she gripped the edge of her writing table for support. Not only was Lady Madderly dead, she'd been murdered, and the murder had taken place in the very recent past. The murderer might still be nearby.

Susanna took a deep, steadying breath. Her fear was irrational. If Eleanor's killer hadn't already been gone by the time she first arrived at the locked door, there had been ample opportunity for him . . . or her . . . to escape when Susanna went for another key. There were any number of places where a person might have been concealed, watching, while she'd juggled those papers and the unwieldy book and her mulled wine.

At the thought, it rose, threatening disaster in an unsettled stomach. Susanna controlled the nausea this time by closing her eyes.

It was not that she had never seen death before. She had been faced with bodies more times than she liked to admit, but they'd usually died of natural causes . . . or of poison. Whatever marks of the last agonizing moments of life remained, they'd never seemed quite as violent as the scene before her. There had never been such a terrible, gaping wound.

Susanna opened her eyes again and stared at the heavy candlestick. There was no doubt that this was the murder weapon.

Only then did she absorb the full impact of the scene.

Someone had murdered Eleanor Madderly.

The same someone who had killed Lord Glenelg?

The possibility was horrifying. If a killer lived in their midst, someone who had killed twice, seemingly at random, then that person might strike again. No one was safe.

And no one was above suspicion.

Susanna felt her face harden into a purposeful mask. Whoever had done this must be found and punished. She would have to call for help soon, and tell Lord Madderly what had happened, but first she would take a closer look at her surroundings. If there was any clue here to the identity of the murderer, she meant to find it.

The room and its contents seemed exactly as they had been an hour and a half earlier.

Except for the silver candlestick and the chilling presence of a murder victim.

And the key.

Susanna's key was missing. It was not on the writing table, which meant that whoever had murdered Lady Madderly had taken it away, using it to lock the door and delay the discovery of the crime.

To be certain it was gone, she scanned the workroom again. Something had fallen, she remembered. Going down on hands and knees, she searched beneath the tables and cabinets. The object Eleanor had been clutching had rolled into a corner. It was not a key, but rather a heavy signet ring. A man's ring.

Susanna picked it up and stood, but before she could take a good look at her prize, a shadow appeared, startling her into making a small sound of alarm. She whirled around, prepared to defend herself against whatever person now filled the open doorway.

Gilbert Russell stood there, his eyes fixed not upon her but on the body.

Susanna quickly secreted the ring in the pouch hidden in her kirtle, never taking her eyes from Gilbert Russell as he skirted Eleanor's remains and moved deeper into the room.

He did not bother with a close examination of the body. He could see at a glance that there was nothing he could do for the dead woman. Instead he turned his suspicious gaze on the one still living.

"Did you kill her, Lady Appleton?" he asked.

10

Catherine Denholm hurried up the inner staircase, tugging her warm wool cloak more tightly about her against the chill. She was glad their trunks had finally arrived, and at nearly the same time a letter sent from Leigh Abbey the day after they'd left. She could hardly wait to tell her mentor, friend, and sister-by-marriage the good news.

Jennet had been safely delivered of another healthy girl, her second in two years. The first she'd named Susanna. This one was to be christened Catherine.

Catherine had never been a godmother before. Even though someone would have to stand in as her proxy at the ceremony, she felt a sense of immense pride that Jennet and her husband, Mark, had asked her to accept the responsibility. Although she could not go herself, she would send gifts. As Susanna had for the first child, Catherine would provide a necklet made of coral, to bring good luck and long life to the baby. And a gift of money. And the promise to care for young Catherine if aught happened to her parents before the child was grown.

A rough place on the twisting, narrow stairs which led to the top of the tower made her slow her pace and with that hesitation came the first doubt. Was that why she'd been chosen? Because she was heiress to the Denholm estate and could provide for the child better than Mark and Jennet could?

Catherine was practical enough to know this was true. She could only hope she'd also been asked to be the child's godmother because Jennet liked her. Leigh Abbey's housekeeper was not always an easy companion, but she was devoted to those she cared about. She would do anything for Susanna.

More slowly now, Catherine continued to climb, uncertainty causing her lips to purse and her fists to clench. Sometimes she had the feeling that she was merely tolerated at Leigh Abbey. This was a familiar torment for which she blamed Sir Robert Appleton. Her half brother did not want to acknowledge their relationship. He had painstakingly explained why it must never even be spoken of, telling her that if she revealed the truth about her birth she would lose her Denholm inheritance.

What Sir Robert failed to say, what Catherine had reasoned out for herself, was that if she did speak out, Robert might lose a portion of *his* estate. No wonder he wanted her to remain silent!

The bitter fact was that Sir Robert had never had any wish to claim her. Susanna had forced him to take Catherine into his home. If he'd been allowed his own way, she would still be moldering in far-off Lancashire . . . or wed these many months to the first wealthy merchant who asked for her hand.

Absorbed by this distressing train of thought, Catherine did not at first realize that the loud voices ahead were coming not from the schoolroom, which she'd already passed without noticing, but from Lady Madderly's workroom. She reached the landing and hesitated there to peer through the open door.

From that angle she could see movement and a flash of crimson. Not Susanna, who had left their rooms before the trunks arrived and was thus still wearing the same dark brown kirtle and hare-color camlet gown in which she'd left Kent. Not Lady Madderly, either, for Catherine had caught a glimpse of her earlier in the day and noticed she was garbed in bright green velvet.

The most likely member of this household to be dressed in that particular shade of crimson was Gilbert Russell. Catherine's smile returned. Perhaps, once she'd delivered her message, she could persuade Master Russell to walk back to the south wing with her. He might even notice that she was wearing different clothing. The peach-colored mocado suited her, she thought, much more than the russet wool she'd been wearing since they arrived.

Catherine started forward only to stop, shocked, when she heard Susanna's voice, sharp with astonishment. "Why in God's heaven would I murder Lady Madderly?" she asked.

Murder?

Catherine gasped, but no one seemed to hear her.

Gilbert Russell's words were clear and clipped. "Aye. Why would you? To put an end to her work, mayhap? 'Tis not a thing I'd kill for, but it seems you are one of the leading herbalists in all of England. Were you jealous? Did you think Lady Madderly's book would surpass your own?"

"If I had killed her, Master Russell, I'd have used poison, and none would ever have suspected aught but a natural death." Susanna's contempt for his suggestion was obvious from her tone.

Silence hung in the workroom following that statement. Catherine had time to creep closer, to look upon the cause of their dispute.

Lady Madderly lay dead. There could be no possible doubt. But how could Gilbert think for one moment that Susanna had done this dastardly deed?

"Lady Appleton studies herbs to save lives, not to take them," she said in a small but carrying voice.

Both turned in her direction. Their mouths moved, but Catherine heard no sound. She saw Susanna start toward her only to be shoved aside. Then Gilbert was right in front of her, blocking her view of the body.

"Go to your chamber," he ordered. "This is no fit sight for a young woman."

She looked up, up, up into his intensely blue eyes. It was suddenly difficult to speak. "I have seen worse," she managed to get out.

Gilbert Russell's face was so close to her own that she could see the fine lines around his eyes and mouth. And she could tell by his frown that he did not believe her. He seized her upper arm and all but dragged her away from the door, finally sitting her down on a cold stone bench cut out of the masonry beneath a window in the passage that went from tower to tower.

"No fainting," he ordered gruffly.

"I never faint," she assured him. "I only *look* frail."

"Get out of the way, you great oaf." Gilbert made a woofing sound as Susanna's elbow rammed into his side on her way past him. "She does not need your assistance, nor your protection from me."

Was he trying to keep her safe? Catherine warmed at the thought. "You are wrong," she told him earnestly. "Lady Appleton would never harm anyone."

"Tell that to my ribs," he muttered.

In her desire to defend her mentor, Catherine was no longer tongue-tied. "Susanna does not commit crimes. Why, in the past she's solved them. Even murder."

His eyebrows lifted. Red-brown, like his hair. "Tell me more, Mistress Denholm. What murder has she been involved in ere now?"

" 'Twas two years past," Catherine said earnestly, "and Susanna nearly died trying to find out the truth."

"Catherine. Enough." The sharpness in Susanna's voice finally got through to Catherine. They'd sworn never to speak of those events in Lancashire, but Catherine could not let Susanna be unjustly accused when she knew her friend was incapable of harming anyone.

"There are matters here that will not wait," Susanna said firmly. "Go you, sir, and raise the hue and cry. The coroner must be sent for, and the justice of the peace. And Lord Madderly must be told that his wife is dead."

"Leave you here alone with the body? I think not. Go you and take her with you." Gilbert jerked his head to indicate Catherine. "Send back the chaplain and the steward. Say nothing of what has happened here until I can speak with Lord Madderly myself."

"And what makes you think you are best suited to deliver such news? Go you and fetch the chaplain. I will remain here. Catherine can make her own way back to our chamber if you think her too delicate a creature to stand guard over a dead woman."

Lady Madderly was dead. Catherine could scarce believe it. Not just dead, but murdered. "Why was she killed?" she asked.

"A good question, lass," Gilbert Russell said.

Impatient, Susanna put her hands on her hips and glared at both of them. "Catherine, this is not the time for questions, especially those which have no immediate answer. If it pleases Master Russell, he and I will remain here while you go and inform the chaplain and the steward. Then go you and find Lord Madderly's sister. She is the proper person to break such dire news to him."

"It does not please Master Russell," Gilbert objected.

Catherine hesitated, uncertain what to do. Then she reached out a hand and placed it on Susanna's arm. "I would be glad of your company," she said in a timid voice.

The look Susanna shot her way was rife with suspicion, but she reluctantly relented. "As you wish." With one last fulminating glare at Gilbert, she led the way to the stairs. "I do not trust that man," she muttered under her breath.

"He does not seem to like you, either." The conclusion was distressing to Catherine. She'd hoped the two of them would learn to appreciate each other in time, for she thought the world of Susanna and she liked Gilbert more than any other man she'd ever met.

Susanna surged ahead, leaving Catherine to follow. She did not speak again until they'd reached the courtyard. Sarcasm laced her words. "You seem recovered from your bout of frailty."

"I feared the two of you would come to blows."

"And so you let him think you a silly creature prone to faint at the sight of blood?"

"I see no harm in that."

"The harm is that I have lost my chance to finish searching that room. And worse, Master Russell remains behind to do as he will." Susanna sounded exasperated.

"What do you think he means to do? Lady Madderly is dead. He cannot harm her more."

Susanna looked up at the tower they had just left. She seemed to be debating with herself. After a moment, she leveled a piercing look in Catherine's direction. "I will not make the mistake of trying to send you to hide in our chamber. Lord Madderly is doubtless in his study. When you have dispatched the steward and the chaplain to the workroom, go to the library. Tell Magdalen Harleigh what has happened and then stay with her until I bring Beatrice. Whatever you do, avoid Gilbert Russell."

With that, she strode away, leaving Catherine to scowl resentfully after her. Catherine's mother had always demanded blind obedience from her daughter. Catherine had not liked being treated like a dull-witted child and left out of things when she was younger. She liked it even less now.

The two years she'd spent with the Appletons had taught her to have confidence in herself. Susanna had been a good and kind friend to her from the moment they met. Moreover, she'd seen to it that Catherine kept full control of her inheritance, even when Sir Robert wanted to meddle in the Denholm estate. She had also made certain that Catherine knew one important fact, that under the law she was free to choose for herself what man she would marry.

Now it seemed that Susanna expected to have a say in how Catherine felt about Gilbert Russell. Susanna did not like him, therefore Catherine must not have anything to do with him. She must yield to Susanna's superior wisdom.

"I am of an age to make mine own decisions," Catherine muttered under her breath. With a defiant toss of her head, she set off toward the library.

11

Lord Madderly was plainly annoyed to answer the knocking at his study door and find his sister and Lady Appleton standing outside. "What is it?" he demanded. He moved so that his bulk blocked Susanna's view of the room behind him.

"Bad news, Henry," Beatrice said. "You had best invite us in."

She sounded calm enough herself. Indeed, Susanna had been surprised by the lack of emotion she'd shown when told of the death of her sister-by-marriage. Beatrice had given Susanna a sharp look, as if to ascertain that she was telling the truth and not participating in some tasteless hoax. Then she'd risen from the high-backed bench where she'd been sitting to work on an embroidered cushion cover and come straight here with Susanna trailing after.

Catherine had already arrived. Therefore Magdalen

knew what had happened. The two of them waited below.

Madderly's scowl deepened as he considered his sister's request. He must have sensed that something serious was afoot but rather than let them in, he came out, carefully closing and locking the door behind him. "Well?"

"It is Eleanor," Beatrice said. "She has been most foully murdered."

"Nonsense."

" 'Tis true, my lord," Susanna said. "I found her so in the tower workroom."

"By Saint Anthony's Fire! Murdered?"

"Aye."

Lord Madderly sank down onto a flat-topped storage chest, eyes glazed and jaw slack. Behind him Magdalen Harleigh appeared with a cup of the same mulled wine she'd pressed on Susanna earlier.

"Drink this," she told him, and it was an indication of how shocked he was that he swallowed the contents of the cup without a murmur of protest.

Her presence momentarily forgotten, Susanna moved to one side of the balcony, near a window where the light was good, and took the opportunity, her first since she'd slipped it into her pouch, to look more closely at the object she'd found clutched in Lady Madderly's hand.

The ring, a man's signet, was made of solid gold and bore the crest of a bee and a thistle. Her first thought was that the thistle was a symbol frequently used in Scottish coats of arms.

Susanna had long had an interest in heraldic matters and could recognize many family emblems and mottoes, but this bee and thistle was unfamiliar to her. It was not Madderly's, though it could be the crest of Eleanor's family. Susanna did not know what her name had been before her marriage.

Or Eleanor could have ripped the circle of gold off her killer's finger.

Susanna closed her hand over the ring and tucked it away once more. The first chance she had, she must write to Robert. She would tell him of Lady Madderly's death. There would be nothing exceptional about a wife sending such news to her husband. She would use that excuse also to ask him to find out the real reason she'd been sent to Madderly Castle.

Whatever his reply, she knew her duty. She must do all she could to uncover the identity of Eleanor's killer.

Of all the members of this household, she could be certain of the innocence of only one. Magdalen Harleigh had been in the library when Susanna arrived there from the tower. Susanna had sat facing the door to work. Thus Magdalen could not possibly have left without being seen. She could not have killed Eleanor Madderly.

It would be an easy task to ascertain where everyone else had been. It was human nature to want to play some small part in any dramatic event. Most people would talk about this horrible crime in hushed whispers and marvel that they had been so near, all unknowing, when it happened. Susanna's expression grew grim. Thus would she narrow her list of suspects.

With a pang of guilt that she should so relish the task before her when this was a house in mourning, Susanna shifted her attention to the grieving widower. The possibility of finding answers excited her, but she would have to use discretion. She must not seem to be asking questions or no one would tell her anything.

The sound of Gilbert Russell's voice reached her before he

appeared at the top of the stairs. She had just time enough to edge into the shadow of the tall, heavy aumbry Lord Madderly used to store illuminated manuscripts of Books of Days. She must be very careful of Gilbert, Susanna warned herself, until she knew why he had turned and followed her after he'd given her the key.

Whence came he before that? Had he murdered Eleanor? This young man who had so conveniently shown up at the murder scene and then had the gall to accuse her of the crime aroused all her darkest suspicions.

Hidden, Susanna gained the opportunity to study Gilbert Russell while he spoke to Lord Madderly. His voice was quiet, but not so faint that she could not overhear him report that all the procedures required by law in a case of murder were being carried out. The bailiff had sent for the coroner and was summoning men for a jury for the inquest.

Their verdict could be in no possible doubt. Once the coroner had examined Eleanor's body, an indictment of homicide was inevitable. But then what would be done? What had been done when Lord Glenelg was killed? Now, as then, there were no obvious suspects.

She'd intended to find out more about Lord Glenelg's murder, but in the last few busy days she'd had few opportunities to investigate. Now she would. With the exception of herself and Catherine, most and perhaps all of the present household must have been in residence when Glenelg was killed. She would pose judicious questions in order to learn who had been in direct contact with the Scots baron and if any of them had clashed with him. She already knew Magdalen Harleigh had. Magdalen had freely admitted it, which once again seemed to proclaim her innocence.

The first focus of her investigation would be Gilbert Russell, Susanna decided. And with good reason. Catherine plainly had feelings for him. It was devoutly to be hoped these were merely the result of a girlish infatuation. With luck, his outrageous accusations had already disillusioned her. If they had not, then there was all the more need to prove Gilbert Russell either guilty or innocent, and quickly, too.

Was there any possible way Gilbert could have killed Lady Madderly and still have encountered Susanna when and where he did? Susanna pondered the question carefully. There had been that sound she'd heard in the passageway. Had that been Master Russell, scurrying away from the scene of the crime?

But if so, why would he return?

And what possible motive could he have had?

Susanna could think of none. Indeed, no one seemed to profit by Eleanor's death, just as no one seemed to have benefited from the murder of Lord Glenelg.

She would have to track Gilbert's every movement, both today and on the day when Lord Glenelg had died. She knew herself to be better than most people at noticing details from which she could piece together a picture of what might have happened. And she had always been able to get people to talk to her.

She decided to begin with the tiring maid, quiet little Nan. Servants always knew more about what was happening in a great house than anyone in the family.

Her chance came two hours later, in the comfort of her own bedchamber. She entered to find Nan inspecting the jars of scent and the trinket boxes that had now joined ivory combs and brushes and the flower vase on the table beneath the looking glass.

" 'Tis glad I am to have caught you, Nan," Susanna said.

Guilt writ large upon her plain-featured face, the tiring maid jumped back from the table and let out a shriek of alarm. Then, recognizing Lady Appleton, she flung her apron up over her head. From beneath its linen folds came a series of whimpers, but she also seemed to be mumbling words. With difficulty, Susanna finally made them out.

"Thee'll larrop I," Nan was saying. "Sure as God's in Glaaster, thee'll larrop I."

A larroping, Susanna presumed, was the local term for a beating. "Calm yourself, Nan. I mean you no harm."

Slowly the apron lowered. Now both hands were pressed over her heart as the wide-eyed girl struggled with conflicting emotions. She clearly wanted to run, but she was duty-bound to stay and see to Lady Appleton's needs.

"I have no plans to, er, larrop you," Susanna said in what she hoped was a reassuring voice. "In truth, I need your help."

When the girl made no reply, Susanna added an inducement. "There will be a reward in it for you if you answer all my questions honestly. Perhaps one of the jars of scent you were just now inspecting?"

"I bean't a-gwaine to steal it."

"I know that, Nan. 'Twas plain you were but admiring these things."

Cautiously, the maidservant began to relax.

"You talk to the other servants, Nan. You hear things. By now everyone must be speculating about Lady Madderly's death. And before that they would have spoken of Lord Glenelg's murder. All I want you to do is repeat what you have heard to me."

"I hire zitch things," Nan acknowledged, "but I doan't talk o' they."

Susanna smiled, a trifle bemused by Nan's strong local accent. When spoken rapidly by a native of these parts, the dialect came close to qualifying as a foreign language. She translated Nan's words without too much difficulty, however, having already observed that here in Gloucestershire people were apt to change *s* to *z* and *f* to *v*. They also tended to add the letter h where it did not belong and to drop the *w* entirely from some words. She'd heard the Cotswolds called Cotsalls more than once since her arrival at Madderly Castle.

"You must talk to me, Nan," Susanna insisted. "What are they saying about this latest murder?"

" 'A bist a madman," Nan mumbled. " 'A came out after she."

"A madman?"

"Bean't true?"

"Likely not."

"Bean't a demon?"

"Most certainly not a demon."

Something of Susanna's confidence seemed to communicate itself to the tiring maid. " 'Tis unkard," she confided.

Susanna took that to mean odd, and smiled in what she hoped was a reassuring way. "Aye," she agreed. "And so the sooner Lady Madderly's murderer is found, the better."

She took Nan by the arm and led her over to the window seat, urging her to sit beside her in front of the casement. Madderly Castle was located in one of the Cotswolds' rare well-wooded valleys, filled with elm, ash, and walnut, and with hazel, beech, and chestnut, but at this time of year the vista before Susanna's eyes was little more than a massing of bare branches. Only the tall firs were still green.

"Now, Nan," she said, turning her attention to the girl at her side, "to find who killed Lady Madderly, we must speak first of the death of Lord Glenelg."

"What happen avoor were naught to do with she," Nan objected.

"Was it not? Well then, Nan, help me prove it so. Tell me all you can recall of the night Lord Glenelg was found murdered in the library."

When the interview concluded some time later, Susanna knew little more than she had before. Nan had only limited contact with any of the gentlemen in the household, though she'd seen enough of Gilbert Russell to describe him as "sprack as a banty-cock."

Nan revealed that she had tried to speak to Lord Glenelg's man, Peadar, after his master's body was discovered. "Zo I zaid to he, 'Be 'ee veeling poorly?'" But Peadar, Nan reported, had been impossible to understand because he had "zuch a unkard furrin manner o' zaying his 'ords."

After Nan left, the richer for a pot of scent and sixpence, Susanna wondered how blatant she dared be in her quest for knowledge. It was one thing to question the servant assigned to take care of her needs, quite another to interrogate the family and their friends. If she offended Lord Madderly, she would be asked to leave. A considerate guest would already have offered to go, rather than become a burden in a house of mourning.

She was still pondering when Catherine bounded into

their bedchamber. Something was afoot. The young woman was unable to suppress the anticipation in her voice. "I have been sent with a message from Lord Madderly," she announced.

"What message?"

"He wishes us to remain here, in spite of the distressing circumstances of his wife's death. He says that there could be no finer tribute to her memory than to complete the herbal she began."

"He wants me to finish it?"

"Aye. He requests that you consider carefully, but he wants your answer by morning."

"He wastes no time."

"He was most secretive about the matter, too. He sent his sister away before he called me to his side to convey this message to you. And he asked for our silence on your decision, that he may announce it to all those concerned."

All those concerned? Only Beatrice and Magdalen would be directly affected. Unkard, as Nan would say.

"Will we be staying?" Catherine asked.

"Have you any doubt? Aye, I will complete Lady Madderly's herbal. 'Tis as worthy a project as ever it was."

Yet conscience tweaked her.

"Can I allow Lord Madderly to think that is my only reason for staying?" she asked. "Or do I owe it to mine host to tell him that I hope to find his wife's murderer?"

"I can think of one good reason to keep silent," Catherine answered.

Susanna had been speaking rhetorically, but she looked to her young friend with interest. "And that is?"

"That Lord Madderly himself is the killer."

12

By the day after Lady Madderly's murder, the coroner's inquest had found a verdict of homicide by persons unknown, the body had been washed with perfumed water, anointed with balsam, encased in a linen shroud, sewn into a deerskin, and placed in a gilded wooden coffin. Magdalen had helped with this process, but she still had difficulty believing Eleanor was dead.

Not that she was allowed to forget for one moment that this was a house in mourning. All the trappings were already in place. Every mirror in the castle had been turned to the wall. Black curtains hung over every window. Every servant had been issued a black gown and hood.

The courtyard and entrance facade of the castle were draped with hangings of black serge, as were the staircase and the first room leading to the great chamber where the coffin stood on a raised dais and juniper and frankincense burned constantly to combat the smell of death. The bier was made of two poles with wooden crosspieces, painted black. Only the pall was not black, but rather made of dark purple velvet and cloth of gold, to indicate the exalted status of the deceased.

When Lord Madderly summoned Magdalen, Beatrice, Lady Appleton, and Mistress Denholm, they gathered in his bedchamber, the accustomed place for a bereaved widower to receive condolences. He sat upright in his mourning bed, a family heirloom reserved for just this purpose. It had been assembled in his chamber as soon as the servants heard of Lady Madderly's death.

Madgdalen stared morosely at the black hangings. It would be a long time before color graced this house again. She would feel that loss more than she would miss Eleanor Madderly.

While they waited for the baron to speak, Magdalen's fingernails strayed to her neck. She caught herself scratching beneath the small ruff and stopped, clasping her hands in front of her. She was not prostrate with grief over the death of her mistress but she was concerned about her own future. Beatrice had never liked her.

She supposed her place in the household was secure as long as Otto was master of horse, but was Otto's position assured? Her husband had been moody of late. More surly in attitude, more disparaging of her interests. He'd never had a good word to say about the things that occupied her time, but until recently he'd at least been an adequate husband in bed. A deep sigh shuddered through Magdalen, embarrassing her when she realized how loud it had sounded in the quiet bedchamber.

Lord Madderly cleared his throat. He was also engulfed in black, attired entirely in black nightclothes. Even the velvet slippers lined up next to the bed were ebony hued.

"I called you here to reassure you," Lord Madderly said. "There have been two murders. No murderer has been caught. In spite of those troubling facts, we have no cause for fear. Lord Glenelg was slain by an old enemy. Naught to do with us. And my wife died at the hands of a thief, an outsider who came to rob her."

Lady Appleton looked as startled by this revelation as Magdalen was. "How do you know this?" she asked.

"Common sense." Lord Madderly looked annoyed at being challenged, an attitude which discouraged any more questions. "The coroner agrees with me," he proclaimed, "as does the local justice of the peace."

Lady Appleton opened her mouth to say more, then shut it again at Lord Madderly's glare.

"Life must go on," Madderly continued, "and I am determined to honor Eleanor's memory. She left a will, of which I am executor. My wife desired that the entire parish be invited to a meal on the Sunday following her funeral and that for it be provided two dozen loaves of bread, a kilderkin of ale, two gammons of bacon, and three shoulders of mutton. A table will be set up in the courtyard. In addition, her will specified that a total of five pounds be distributed to the poor."

How generous of Eleanor, Magdalen thought. And hardly like her. No doubt this was an attempt to buy salvation. In the old days when England was a Catholic country, the poor would have prayed for her soul in return for their money. Now they were merely expected to wish her well on her journey into the afterlife.

"My wife was engaged in the compilation of a great work. This must be finished, even though she is no longer here to guide it. To that end I have asked Lady Appleton to go forward with the preparation of the herbal. I will expect each of you to assist her in any way she requires."

A fleeting expression of outrage crossed Beatrice's face before she got control of her emotions. Though Beatrice now presented an impassive countenance to the world, Magdalen was not deceived. Beatrice resented her brother's decision. She thought she should be the one in charge of everything.

Magdalen smoothed one hand over her black brocade sleeve, secretly delighting in the feel of the fine fabric. Beatrice's gown might be grander, as suited her higher station, but Magdalen's was most luxuriant.

From beneath lowered eyelids she surreptitiously examined Lady Appleton's attire and that of her young companion, Catherine Denholm. 'Twas good luck for them that their trunks had arrived, and better still that they were not obliged to dress entirely in black, since Eleanor had been neither mistress nor kin to them.

"That is all I have to say," Lord Madderly concluded. "I would be alone in my grief."

"And I would have a word with you in private, brother." Beatrice's tone was frosty.

Magdalen gladly followed Lady Appleton from the room. She had no desire to overhear the Madderlys quarreling.

"I approve of this plan to finish the herbal," Magdalen said when they were well away. "Will you begin at once?"

"Aye, though 'twill be difficult at first without Eleanor's guidance. I never did discern her overall plan."

"It may be contained in her notebooks."

Lady Appleton looked surprised. "What notebooks?"

"They should be in her workroom. Lady Madderly told me she'd been making extensive notes on the arrangement of her herbal, lists of the plants she meant to include, organized by their uses."

"Did you see these notes for yourself?"

Magdalen managed a faint smile. "Not I. For, as you know, Eleanor preferred to reveal only that information pertinent to the task at hand."

"An unfortunate habit," Lady Appleton mused. "I must look at these notebooks as soon as possible."

"There is a standing-box in the workroom," Magdalen told her. "It is made of spruce and pine wood and hasped with steel. That is where Eleanor filed letters and papers and may be where she kept her notebooks, too."

"My thanks." Lady Appleton started to bustle away, then turned back. "Would you care to come with me?"

Magdalen readily agreed. There was no body in the work-room now, and no bloodstains remained. Beatrice had over-seen a thorough cleaning as soon as the coroner had viewed the scene.

Lady Appleton did not seem pleased by the other woman's efficiency. "At least she put everything back in place, except the papers and books upon which Lady Madderly was lying."

Taken aback by this statement, Magdalen hesitated in the doorway. As she watched, Lady Appleton opened the standing-box and lifted out several leather-bound notebooks.

"It was not locked," Magdalen said in surprise.

"So I noticed. Which means we have no way of telling if anything is missing. Do you know what is supposed to have been stolen by Eleanor's murderer?"

Magdalen shook her head. Something in the other woman's tone reinforced Magdalen's earlier impression that Lady Appleton disagreed with Lord Madderly's claims. It did not surprise her, though, that neither of them had voiced their dissention aloud. Lord Madderly's castle was a small kingdom and he was its absolute ruler. If Lady Appleton wished to stay and complete Eleanor's herbal, she must give the appearance of accepting the dictates of the head of the household.

Turning with one of the notebooks in her hand, Lady Appleton smiled and waved Magdalen into the workroom. "Come and sit," she invited. "I need your assistance in another matter."

Magdalen obeyed, as much from her own inclination as from force of habit. Lady Appleton took the stool opposite, her body tilted slightly forward so that she gave the impression of being about to confide something of importance.

"You have already told me of your encounter with Lord Glenelg the day he died," she said. "Who else saw him in the library that day?"

Surprised by the question, Magdalen nevertheless answered readily, telling Lady Appleton of Glenelg's encounters with the two boys, with Beatrice, and with John Wheelwright, the tutor. Halfway through the account she realized she was scratching her arm again, and just when it had seemed to be healing.

"What do you know about how he died?" Lady Appleton asked.

"He was stabbed. In the heart. And the knife was taken away."

"There must have been a great deal of blood, then."

"Why, no." She had seen the floor on the balcony for herself soon after the murder, but until now had not thought it curious there was no stain.

"Then the knife was likely removed after he had been dead for a time," Lady Appleton concluded.

Magdalen nodded slowly. She remembered once seeing a deer that had been killed by a bowman. When the arrow was removed, several hours after the animal's death, the only blood had been a small smear on the arrowhead.

"Did you see Eleanor yesterday?" Lady Appleton asked.

Magdalen gave her a hard look. "You think the same person killed both Lord Glenelg and Lady Madderly."

"Yes, I do. Will you help me prove it?"

"I do not see how I can."

"You might start by answering my question."

"We took breakfast together, ale and bread, in her bedchamber." Magdalen heaved a great sigh. "Then I went off to the library, where you saw me later yourself, and she said she was going to meet you in her workroom."

"Did you break your fast together every day?"

"Aye."

"Thus you would have noticed if something was upsetting her. Did she behave normally that morning?"

Magdalen hesitated. "Why, I suppose so. It was not her wont to confide in me, but since I have worked closely with her for several years, I think I would have sensed agitation or anger."

"Or fear?"

"She was not afraid. Why would she be? She could not have known what the day would bring."

"But she may have known she would be meeting with a

killer. Lord Madderly's theory of a thief as murderer is absurd. Whoever killed Eleanor was someone she knew, and likely the same person who killed Lord Glenelg."

"What of Lord Madderly's claim that an old enemy killed Glenelg?"

"That may be true, but even if it is, that enemy is here among us. Nothing else makes sense." She reached into the deep placket in her kirtle and withdrew a small object. "When Eleanor died, she was clutching this in her hand. Have you ever seen it before?"

Magdalen took the heavy gold signet ring and held it up to the light. Startled by what she saw, she nearly dropped it. Her hands began to shake and her heart beat faster.

"The crest is the same as on Lord Glenelg's bye-knife! The one he was wont to clean his fingernails with, and gesture with, too." She blanched, remembering how near to her own nose it had once come. And then another thought turned her face even more pale. "It could have been the very weapon that was used to kill him!"

"This crest, this bee and thistle, was on a knife Lord Glenelg owned?"

"Aye. It was."

Lady Appleton looked pleased to have her theory confirmed and at the same time deeply troubled. "Say nothing of this to anyone, Magdalen," she warned. "Someone who has killed twice will find it far too easy to kill again."

13

sing the proverb frequently spoken by those who enter upon dangerous and bold attempts, he took the river. What proverb?" the boys' tutor asked.

"*Iacta alea est,*" Edward answered.

The die is cast, Susanna silently translated as she crossed the threshold of the schoolroom. Spoken languages besides her own were a trial to her, but she could manage quite well with written words and her father had taught her Latin from Plutarch's *Lives* when she was younger than Philip Madderly. "He" was Julius Caesar. The river was the Rubicon.

"Master Wheelwright," she interrupted. "A word with you?"

If he was annoyed to have the lesson disrupted, he concealed it well. After a brief delay to give instructions to his two young charges, work enough to keep them busy while he was otherwise occupied, Wheelwright joined her near the door.

The ferret wrapped around his shoulders regarded her with a bright, beady stare. Wheelwright's dark eyes were also intense, but had a less disconcerting effect. "How may I be of assistance, Lady Appleton?"

"I am most concerned," she said in a confiding tone. "This thief Lord Madderly says killed his wife. What if the man returns? How would any of us recognize him?"

"I do not know, Lady Appleton."

"You might have heard him pass by on his way to the workroom. Perhaps you caught a glimpse of him?"

Wheelwright ran long, thin fingers over the point of his short chin beard. "I heard Lady Madderly go up that morning, and a short time later I believe you joined her, Lady Appleton. Then you went back out."

"And after that?"

"After that I was too involved with my work to notice."

"Perhaps the boys saw something?"

"No chance of it. We were engaged in a . . . training exercise." He cleared his throat and looked away. "Perhaps I'd best confess. It was more of a game. Involving blindfolds. So you see, none of us could have noticed anything."

Susanna felt a flicker of sympathy for him. Though she approved of occasional play to relieve the tedium of study, no self-respecting schoolmaster would want it widely known that he'd been engaged in a game of blind-man's buff when his employer was being murdered on the floor above.

"What did you do after your . . . training exercise?" she asked.

"We went out to the archery butts. No game, that," he

added defensively. "Teaching the boys to shoot with bow and arrow is part of my commission here."

Diversity was admirable in a schoolmaster, Susanna thought, noting for the first time that Wheelwright was lean but well muscled. Though past his prime by the gray in his hair, he was as yet unaffected by any of the more common signs of aging.

Susanna could not help but admire good health. 'Twas a rare commodity. It also signified that this man had been well cared for from the cradle. Likely he was some gentleman's younger son, down on his luck.

"It grieves me I can offer no better reassurance," Wheelwright said. One hand went up to stroke Bede, who was growing restless in his role as a collar.

The comment reminded Susanna that she was supposed to be playing the role of frightened female, and she belatedly realized Catherine would have been better suited to the part. It took a good deal of effort to sound as if she needed a man to tell her she'd be safe at Madderly Castle.

"Do you think the killer was a thief, someone who crept in unseen and is long gone by now?"

"What other explanation can there be?" Wheelwright asked.

Susanna leaned close and lowered her voice. "Some supernatural fiend," she whispered. "Or so some of the servants say. A demon." For good measure, she added, "Conjured up by witches."

"My dear Lady Appleton!" John Wheelwright pulled away from her, drawing himself up stiffly and shifting the ferret from his shoulder to his arms. "That is naught but superstitious nonsense. No educated man believes in such things."

She smiled as she took her leave, for she agreed with him completely.

Four days after Lady Madderly's murder, Susanna sat alone in the workroom. In that time, her investigation had only succeeded in raising more unanswered questions.

Everyone in the family and among the upper servants save Magdalen Harleigh seemed content to accept the absurd claim that two separate outsiders had entered the castle without anyone noticing their presence and done murder. Nan's theory about the demon made as much sense!

Susanna had made one futile attempt to talk to the authorities, but both the coroner and the justice of the peace were anxious to go along with Lord Madderly, especially after he claimed that a pouch of gold coins had been taken from Eleanor's workroom. Susanna suspected a craven desire to please the local nobility had a great deal to do with their willingness to believe him.

Susanna wondered if Robert had received the letter she'd sent three days earlier. She supposed not. It had not qualified to go by packet, the official mail sent on at once by post-relay. Instead it had been dispatched in the form of a bye-letter, which meant it must sit and wait for forwarding at each posting place along the way until the next packet came through. Only then was it added to a postboy's mailbag.

She might have done better to send a running footman from the Madderly staff, but she hadn't wanted to arouse suspicion. This must appear to be no more than an ordinary communication from wife to husband.

Meanwhile, she must plod along unaided. She did not feel she had accomplished much besides questioning Nan and

Magdalen and Master Wheelwright. Her second effort with the schoolmaster had yielded only a denial that he'd ever quarreled with Lord Glenelg. He claimed he'd gone to the library that day only to return the book his young charges had taken from Magdalen. He insisted, too, that Glenelg had accosted him, wanting to know what was in Lord Madderly's study.

Susanna wondered herself.

Wheelwright said he'd been unable to assist the Scots baron and had been quick to use his waiting pupils as an excuse to escape Glenelg's company. Susanna did not doubt it. But had Wheelwright harbored a grudge? Had he gone back later and killed Lord Glenelg?

'Twas as likely the ferret had done it! Susanna could think for no reason why either would want Glenelg dead, let alone Eleanor.

Shaking her head, she went to her worktable. She would compose a second letter to Robert, as much for her own benefit as his. Perhaps it would help clarify what she'd learned if she wrote it down. She'd also ask him to verify her conclusion that the bee and thistle was Lord Glenelg's family crest.

The paper provided for letters at Madderly Castle was thick, ivory-colored stock imported from Antwerp. Deckle-edged, it had the watermark of a hand and flower. She speculated that it had cost at least four shillings a ream.

It was pure pleasure to write upon such stuff. Susanna dipped her quill into a pewter inkwell and began to form satisfyingly bold dark letters.

"Gilbert Russell," she wrote a few minutes later, then tapped the feather end of the quill against her lower lip. An enigma. He still behaved as if he thought she might have killed Eleanor Madderly. Susanna wondered if he was doing the same thing she was. Asking questions. Looking for answers. If so, was he having as much difficulty? Was that why he continued to suspect her?

And why, she asked herself, did she still suspect him? Mostly because she could not clear him of either murder. Neither could she find anything to indicate he had a motive for wanting either victim dead. Catherine had mentioned seeing him leave the castle late one night, but the likely explanation for that was a willing wench on some nearby farm.

"Magdalen Harleigh," she wrote next. Impossible for her to have killed Eleanor, but even though she'd volunteered the information about the crest, she *had* quarreled with Lord Glenelg. Had Glenelg threatened her in some way? Magdalen was certainly nervous enough to be keeping a dark secret. What was she trying to hide?

"Otto Harleigh" was the next name inscribed on the page. A husband might act in concert with a wife. Had one killed Glenelg, the other Eleanor because she'd found out?

Continuing to write down everything she knew, little as it was, Susanna turned next to Beatrice Madderly. She had quarreled with Lord Glenelg the day he died. And shown little emotion at the news of Eleanor's death. Beatrice had so far also deftly deflected all of Susanna's efforts to draw her into conversation.

"John Wheelwright." Though none seemed important, Susanna enumerated each of their encounters and told Robert about Bede, the ferret.

That brought her to Lord Madderly.

Susanna stopped and considered. What possible motive could he have had for killing both a guest in his home and his own wife? An affair between Eleanor and Glenelg seemed unlikely. Yet Madderly was clearly attempting to place the blame on strangers, which was suspicious in itself.

Her questions to him would have to wait until after the funeral, and would have to be subtle even then. If he was protecting the memory of his wife as well as attempting to avoid notoriety, he would not want any connection to be established between the two murders.

An errant thought had Susanna adding another name— Lady Madderly's. It was not impossible that Eleanor should have killed Lord Glenelg, for some as yet unknown reason. What if she had? And what if someone had then killed her to avenge him?

In truth, she knew little about the dead woman. Part of what she had learned in recent days had shocked her. Eleanor's "great work" turned out to be sadly lacking in greatness. Her notebooks were disorganized. At least one seemed to be missing. Worse, those Susanna had examined contained numerous mistakes.

How could any good herbalist confuse sassafras with saxifrage? The former came from the New World. Its bark was believed to be a sovereign remedy for the pox. The latter was a fern. Most commonly its roots were steeped in the blood of a hare, then baked and powdered. The end product, taken morning and night, was a popular treatment for the stone.

More alarming still, Eleanor had written that an infusion of one ounce of dried wormwood to one pint of boiling water, taken in doses of two ounces three times a day, would bring down a woman's courses. Susanna's own experience told her that would be good advice if one used wormwood's cousin, southernwood, but such large doses of wormwood, long continued, would most assuredly have serious ill effects on the body. A woman following Eleanor's advice ran the risk of inducing convulsions.

Susanna did not bother to share her discouraging conclusions about Eleanor's scholarship with Robert. Instead she penned the suggestion that he find and talk to Lord Glenelg's man, Peadar. Mayhap he could shed some light on the Scot's relationship to those at Madderly Castle.

Writing an account of what she knew had led her to no new conclusions, but Susanna felt a little better as she blotted the ink, folded her letter into a thin oblong packet, and wrote Robert's name and the location of his lodgings in Edinburgh, recently provided to her by Walter Pendennis, on the outside.

Had she omitted any suspects? Lord Madderly's two children came to mind. She had seen little of them, but had heard a great deal to their discredit from Magdalen. On one occasion, when obliged to serve as pages at their father's table, Edward and Philip had impregnated a wet napkin with powdered vitriol and gall and induced Eleanor to wipe her hands with it. When her fingers turned black as a result, the boys had been banished to the schoolroom for meals. Exactly what they'd hoped for, Susanna surmised. Although she could easily imagine the two of them plotting other similar mischief, accusing them of murder seemed far-fetched.

The chaplain? Steward? Cook? One of the lower servants? Less likely still. What profit in taking such a risk?

Outsiders? Two separate killers? Let the authorities investigate that faint possibility, since they were so determined to believe that was what had happened. Let them search for the mythical pouch of gold coins Lord Madderly said his wife always kept in her workroom. Susanna did not believe the tale. There had been no reason for Eleanor to do such a foolish thing, and no one but Lord Madderly claimed to have known such a pouch existed.

The scarlet sealing wax was heated. Susanna dropped it onto sealing thread and pressed down with her own small signet ring. Someone in this household had a motive that explained everything, a reason to kill both victims. All Susanna had to do, she thought as she stared down at the the Appleton crest of an apple pierced through with an arrow, was uncover it.

14

Five days after the murder, Lady Madderly's funeral procession set out from Madderly Castle. Lord Madderly, as was the custom, stayed behind in his bed. Beatrice Madderly was chief mourner, her train carried by Magdalen Harleigh, assisted by Gilbert Russell. He was so handsome, Catherine thought. Black suited him nearly as well as crimson.

Catherine was well back in the crowd making its way over some four miles of ground that Nan called "scrumpety" from the first severe frost. Their goal was Campden, which Susanna had said was a bustling, wool-trading market town. It lay in a fold in the hills and Catherine's first sight of it was the pinnacle of St. James, where Eleanor Madderly was to be buried. She saw the whole of the church, its exterior a rich brown color, as soon as they entered Campden's long, wide High Street, which terminated at the house of worship.

Along the way were a number of buildings of honey-colored local stone. One dwelling had a fine paneled bay window two stories high.

As she passed by an impressive Woolstapler's Hall and its adjacent warehouses, Catherine had to remind herself she was not in Campden to gawk at the sights. This was a somber occasion, and an impressive display of Lord Madderly's importance in these parts. Not only were all the members of the Madderly household in the cortege, but also the mayor of Campden and his brethren and the choir of St. James, singing solemnly. Heralds preceded the coffin. Numerous gentlemen and gentlewomen of the town had joined neighborhood gentry at the end of the procession. Last of all came an even hundred poor men and women, the almsfolk, each of whom had been given a black cloth gown and paid twopence to weep and wail.

Catherine forgot her resolution again when she got her first look at the interior of the church. It was wonderful to behold, especially the floor, all paved with black and white marble. Equally impressive were the oaken benches carved with the arms, or sometimes the marks, of wealthy wool staplers.

Reluctantly, Catherine forced her gaze to focus on the coffin and remember why she was there. Bunches of yew and rosemary had been tied to the sides. They were supposed to be emblems of the soul's immortality.

The widower's chaplain preached a long-winded sermon, but eventually the service was over and Lady Madderly was lowered into the crypt beneath the choir. Once it was closed, the congregation filed past. Every mourner carried a small bunch of bay and rosemary and now threw these evergreens onto the flat gravestone set into the marble floor. Before long

114

it was mounded high with flowers and garlands. An impressive memorial, Catherine thought, soon to be replaced by a more permanent one, an elaborate brass installed in the slab in Lady Madderly's memory.

Back at Madderly Castle, food and drink were served, a great feast of cold meats, biscuits, sweets, and wine for all who would come, even though another such grand repast was planned for Sunday. In the great chamber the distinguished guests sat down to a dinner presided over by the chief mourner. To Beatrice, too, fell the task of handing out presents. Scarves and gloves were given to friends and relatives, sixty pairs of the latter, or so Catherine had heard. She got a pair herself. Other mourners received gifts of money.

Susanna, Catherine noticed, was very quiet throughout the formalities. Only after dinner, when she found herself standing to one side with Magdalen Harleigh and Catherine, did she make any comment. "There were no kinfolk here from Eleanor's family. Has she no living relatives?"

"Eleanor was born a Radcliffe of Elnestow," Mistress Harleigh said.

"Where is Elnestow?" Catherine asked. Radcliffe was a common name in Lancashire, but she had not heard of Elnestow.

"Bedfordshire." Susanna looked thoughtful. "That is not so very far away, which makes it odder still that no one came to represent the family. The Radcliffes of Elnestow," she added for Catherine's benefit, "are a cadet branch of the family of the earl of Sussex."

"Eleanor rarely spoke of her past," Magdalen told them, "but she once confided to me that she was the child of a first marriage and that her father's second wife resented her."

As Eleanor Madderly herself had resented her husband's two sons, Catherine thought. She had spent some time of late with Edward and Philip and their schoolmaster. And his ferret.

"I think," Susanna murmured when Mistress Harleigh had drifted away, "that we might consider making a journey to Bedfordshire."

15

EDINBURGH

Sir Robert Appleton scowled as he noticed that his wife's second letter from Madderly Castle was lying open on the table. He glanced quickly at his mistress, but Annabel, wandering about his bedchamber to admire his possessions, seemed unaware of his disquiet. She wore nothing but a knitted petticoat imported from the Low Countries, his most recent gift to her.

He'd accumulated a fair number of nice things since his arrival in Edinburgh, Annabel herself among them. He saw no reason not to acquire luxuries. He expected to be in Scotland for some time to come. Tom Randolph might be Queen Elizabeth's official ambassador, but Robert could provide the Crown with other valuable services.

His bed hangings were of yellow satin with scarlet fringe. The linen sheets came from Dowlas in Brittany. The window cloths were black and yellow say. The wooden trencher which held the remains of their meal was made of polished beechwood. The wineglasses were imported from Murano, the glass powdered in gold dust, the bowls as shallow as a leaf, and the stems blown into delicate lion masks.

"My queen is more fair," Annabel murmured in French. She was studying the portrait of Queen Elizabeth hanging against the wainscotted inner wall.

As far as Robert could see, there was little to distinguish the two women, certainly not in their contrariness. Queen Elizabeth had kept him dancing to a merry tune of her own devising ever since the beginning of her reign. Always she held out the possibility of his elevation to the peerage, luring him into spending his own money on her behalf. Queen Mary was younger. Prettier. Less given to fits of temper. But she wanted Vanguard. She tolerated Robert at her court, alternately teasing him and ignoring his presence, ever hopeful that he would offer to bribe her with that which she desired.

From time to time he wondered if she knew of his relationship with Annabel and encouraged it. The queen's lady would have made an ideal intelligence gatherer in the English camp but for the singular fact that she had no skill at dissembling. Her every thought was there to read in a pretty, vapid face.

"You are fairer far than any queen," Robert told his mistress, also speaking in French. "And as you well know, I have a weakness for redheaded lasses."

Pleased, she cast a flirtatious glance in his direction, then moved on to examine a sea picture he'd recently purchased. At the same time, he had acquired one of Clement Ames's cuts of Master Sebastian Cabot's map of the world. He'd hung that in the outer room.

Thinking of the map reminded him again of Susanna's letter. Soon he was going to have to leave Edinburgh. Sooner than he'd intended. Annabel would not be pleased.

He considered not telling her, but that would only delay the inevitable. Besides, it was possible Annabel might know something of this mysterious Lord Glenelg who had so inconveniently gotten himself murdered at Madderly Castle.

To date, Robert had not been able to learn much about the man. His family name was Ferguson and they hailed from Dunfallandy. He'd been the eighth baron, having succeeded his father some ten years back. And as a young man, Niall Ferguson had supported the Catholic faction now out of favor in Scotland. Had his activities at Madderly Castle been part of a papist plot to undermine the alliance between the English queen and Scots protestants?

Susanna had written of one Peadar, Lord Glenelg's man, but short of a long journey to the wild and untamed land north and west of the Firth of Tay, there was little likelihood of locating the fellow. If Peadar did not want to be found, such a trip would be in vain. Since that part of Scotland was Gaelic-speaking, Robert doubted he'd even be able to make his wishes known to the locals, let alone secure their cooperation against one of their own.

Better to stay here and do what he could. "Have you ever heard of Lord Glenelg?" he asked Annabel.

Startled by the question, she turned to face him. "The old baron or the new?"

"The one who died not long ago."

"I did not know him."

"And the new baron."

"No one knows him."

"Explain."

"I have heard no one has been able to locate the heir. The old baron's nephew. He is in England somewhere."

"England?" This was unexpected. "Why?"

"Because he is half English." She giggled, delighted that she'd managed to surprise him. "His Scots mother ran off and married a handsome Englishman."

Annabel moved very close to Robert to run one hand over the line of his beard and up to caress his cheek. "I do think all Englishmen are most handsome." She changed the caress into a light slap. "But why do you ask me questions about this minor lord when there are so many much better ways to spend our time?"

Robert debated the wisdom of lying, then decided against it. "Lord Glenelg was murdered at Madderly Castle. Now Lady Madderly has also been slain and I have been asked to look into the matter."

"Why you?"

No help for it, Robert decided. "Because my lady wife is a guest there. She was helping Lady Madderly prepare an herbal for publication."

Annabel already knew Susanna was the author of *A Cautionary Herbal.* Not only had she seen the inscribed copy he'd brought with him to Scotland, but two years ago, in France, Annabel had been the one sent to him late one night with the gift of a recipe for an antidote against poison. She'd brought it to him from no less a person than Catherine de Medici, the Queen Mother. At the time, Mary Stewart had been married to the French king, Catherine's son Francis.

For just an instant, something very like jealousy flickered in Annabel's eyes. A moment later, though, Robert decided he must have imagined it. Annabel was smiling sweetly at him. "For certain you must go," she said. She kissed him lightly. "The sooner you do, the sooner you will come back to me."

Relieved, Robert returned the kiss. "You are wise beyond your years, *ma belle*. I must leave within the week if I am to be in Gloucestershire by Saint Nicholas's Day."

"Such haste!" she exclaimed. "Do you fear your wife may be murdered, too?"

At the blatantly hopeful note in her voice, he had to chuckle. "Perhaps I fear she will beat me if I do not come quickly enough."

Annabel whispered a bawdy rejoinder into his ear.

16

MADDERLY CASTLE

be wappered," Catherine declared as she flung herself down upon the bed and assumed a pose that denoted complete exhaustion.

"Have you been spending time with our Nan again?" Susanna asked. She turned away from the window and her solemn contemplation of the night. Nan would say it was "black as the devil's nutting bag" out there.

"Nay, I have not." Catherine yawned loudly.

"Wappered?"

With a laugh, Catherine sat up and hugged her knees to her chest. "Edward and Philip," she explained. "They possess a whole storehouse of knowledge."

"Is any of it to our purpose? The murders, I mean."

Susanna's frustration grew with each passing day. Nearly two weeks had elapsed since the funeral of Lady Madderly and she did not feel she was one step closer to finding out who had murdered her. Her only new discovery had been a hidden door in the library. She was not sure that had significance, save that no one had troubled to mention it to her. Not even Magdalen.

The door was a possible escape route for Lord Glenelg's killer. Had it also allowed Magdalen to slip out and murder Eleanor Madderly while Susanna had been engaged in searching for *The Secrets of Alexis*?

"Is anything to our purpose?" Catherine asked.

"I do wonder. I accomplish precious little. I did not even prevail in the argument over the organization of Eleanor's herbal."

"Does that debate yet rage?" Catherine had ceased to assist the other women more than a week earlier, when Beatrice had once again deemed her presence unnecessary.

Susanna did not understand why Beatrice had taken such a dislike to Catherine. The girl was young, pretty, and unmarried, and attracted male attention Beatrice might prefer to reserve for herself, but if jealousy was behind the older woman's attitude, it would have made more sense to require Catherine to spend all her time in the workroom. Instead, she'd been turned loose in the castle.

"Beatrice," Susanna said, "still feels the herbs should be categorized by the ailments they soothe, ignoring the fact that most herbs are used for more than one purpose. She points out that this was Eleanor's plan. Magdalen agrees with me that an alphabetical arrangement makes more sense, but she wants to call the plants by their Latin names, which most goodwives will not recognize."

Susanna could see some merit in this system, since many plants went by various names in different parts of the land, but argued that the most common one should be chosen and the others cross-referenced.

"Beatrice Madderly is a selfish cow," Catherine declared.

Susanna fought a smile. Since having Catherine free to gossip with servants and others in the household suited her own purposes so admirably, she'd voiced no objections when Beatrice demanded the girl be banished from the workroom. Catherine, though, had resented Beatrice's attitude and now returned her animosity in full measure.

"She is ugly, too," Catherine added. "If I had such a nasty birthmark at the pit of my throat, I'd be more careful to keep it covered."

This time Susanna could not restrain herself and Catherine must have seen her lips twitch.

"What is so amusing?" she demanded.

"That 'nasty birthmark' is a love bite, Catherine. 'Tis likely Beatrice is indulging in a bit of subtle bragging." She'd also, Susanna realized, been wearing a smug, secretive smile for the last few days.

"Love—you mean some man did that to her? She has a lover?"

"Aye."

"How disgusting!" But Catherine's face worked as she considered this new and fascinating aspect of human behavior. Susanna watched her outrage fade into curiosity, then abruptly change to embarrassment.

To give the girl time to recover her composure, Susanna once more studied the landscape. Through the open window, the music of the night reached her ears. She recognized the cry of the nightjar and the distant sound of foxes barking. "Such an odd noise," she murmured.

"Yoppeting," Catherine supplied. "Foxes yoppeting." The eerie scream of an owl underscored her words and she grinned. "And that be a scritch-owl. Did you know they say *ship* for sheep hereabout? 'Tis most confusing."

"Not when you consider that there are no deepwater ports near at hand." But Susanna had been puzzled herself when she'd first heard Nan refer to a shipvold.

"Edward and Philip have been teaching me some of the odder expressions," Catherine told her. "We did laugh and laugh when we tried to speak like Nan does. It was all we could do to say we were zitting by the vire, listening for the 'oodpecker in the 'ood." She giggled, remembering.

"Have a care, Catherine. You are perilous close to insulting these good people."

"But it does sound so funny."

"So did you before you left Lancashire." Susanna had undertaken to replace her young charge's regional accent with the true kind of pronunciation used at court. A rustic dialect could make anyone a laughingstock.

Chastened, Catherine hastily changed the subject. "You have just spent another day closeted with Beatrice Madderly and Magdalen Harleigh. Did you have any success in questioning them about the murders?"

"Neither woman is inclined to speak of them," Susanna said glumly, "not even out of the other's presence. And we are kept perilous busy finding and correcting errors in Eleanor's research."

Eleanor had insisted that each entry contain a description of the herb, an account of the places where it grew, the names it was called in different parts of England, and the virtues it possessed. When it came to prying recipes out of the local cunning women and midwives, no one had been Eleanor's equal. One of her sources, old Mother Coddington, had proved a font of knowledge. Unfortunately, in order to consolidate information from a variety of sources, it was also necessary to consult ancient texts such as the writings of Pliny and more recent books of healing, many of which were available only in German. Eleanor had lacked the language skills necessary for that task. Some of her mistakes were amusing, others potentially deadly. All had to be caught and corrected. This painstaking process now occupied so much of Susanna's time that she had little opportunity to investigate other matters.

"So, my eyes and ears," she said to Catherine, "what have you heard in the rest of the castle?"

"I do not know how Beatrice can be such a trouble to you," Catherine complained. "She seems to find ample time to follow me about. More than once she has appeared at my elbow at a most inconvenient time. Only in the schoolroom am I certain of being free of her scrutiny. Beatrice despises her nephews."

"So you have nothing to report?"

"I did not say that. I did learn something today, besides the proper way to carve a piece of wood into the shape of an animal." Catherine left the bed and joined Susanna at the window. "I know now why Lady Madderly's family did not attend her funeral."

"They are estranged, or so Magdalen told us weeks ago."

"Aye, but the story is most romantic."

Susanna lifted a skeptical brow, but nodded for Catherine to continue.

"It was during the reign of Henry VIII," Catherine said.

"The earl of Sussex, the old earl, that is, and his second son, Sir Humphrey, Eleanor's father, rode out of London to take part in a tournament. They passed through a small village on their way, and their cavalcade attracted the attention of all the villagers, especially one young woman who was a visitor in that place. She leaned so far out a window in her eagerness to see the knights that she dropped her glove just as Sir Humphrey Radcliffe passed by. Sir Humphrey dipped his lance, impaled the glove, and held it up for its owner to take back. And in that moment, the girl's beauty cast a spell on Sir Humphrey. He could not forget her. Instead of going on to the tournament, he returned to the village. There he found the girl and her father, a prosperous merchant, were about to set out for London. Sir Humphrey told them he was a mere squire in the service of the earl and offered them his protection for the journey. Naturally, his offer was accepted. Then, when they reached the merchant's house, Sir Humphrey was invited to stay and sup with the family."

"And obviously fell in love and married. I assume the girl had a large dowry to make up for her lack of birth?"

"You have no romance in your soul," Catherine complained.

"Did she?"

"Yes!"

"Hah!"

"But it was a love match. Master Wheelwright says she did not know until after the wedding that her new husband was the son, rather than the servant, of the earl of Sussex."

"No doubt her father did." Susanna smiled to take away some of the cynicism of the remark, but she did not care for Catherine's dreamy-eyed look.

"It proved a most happy union, for all but the child of Sir Humphrey's first marriage."

"Eleanor Madderly. Yes, I can see how a stepmother from the merchant class would grate on her."

"I do feel sorry for her," Catherine admitted, "though I am glad for the happiness of Sir Humphrey and his Isabelle. That was her name. Isabelle. They were blessed with several children and then there was no room for the older daughter."

"Still, 'tis odd no one came to see her buried, for all that they were estranged."

And something else bothered her, now that the names Isabelle and Humphrey had been spoken. Then she remembered. It was a story Robert had told her just after the Yuletide season last year. A girl had been presented by her father, in jest, as the queen's New Year's gift and ended up as a maid of honor. Surely Robert had said that she was the daughter of Sir Humphrey Radcliffe of Elnestow.

Robert, Susanna remembered, had given the queen a pair of sleeves and a partlet wrought with gold, silver, and black silk. It had been far too expensive a gift from one of his rank. Worse, he had received no special favor for it. The queen had been far more impressed with the silk stockings she'd received from Mrs. Montagu, her silkwoman, even to the point of swearing to henceforth wear no more stockings of cloth.

Susanna wondered what Robert intended to bestow upon the queen this year. Not the identity of a killer. That seemed certain.

He should have responded to her first letter by now, and received the second. She could only hope he was acting on the requests they contained, in particular that he had gone in search of Peadar, Lord Glenelg's man.

17

Robert followed the Warwick road and Kingcombe
Plain to Campden and then rode along the windy,
less-traveled uplands of the Cotswolds toward Madderly Castle. The wolds themselves appeared to him to be
naught but vast sheep walks, and he'd never cared much for
sheep.

He arrived, precisely as he'd intended, in the evening on
the sixth day of December, only to find that his wife was not
expecting him and was not particularly pleased by his sudden
reappearance in her life. There was no time to speak pri-
vately with her before supper, and afterward she informed
him she had work to finish and disappeared into some distant
tower of Madderly Castle with the other women.

Lord Madderly was not welcoming, either, though both
the season and good manners obliged him to offer Robert his

hospitality. As soon as the meal was over, he locked himself in his private study. Robert had a choice between sitting in the hall with the servants and retiring to the chamber Susanna had been using.

His mood bleak as the landscape, he waited there, contemplating what it would mean to spend Yuletide in a house of mourning. Surely there would be some festivities, even if they were subdued, but there would be nothing like the gaiety of the royal court, Elizabeth's or Mary's. The prospect of spending the next few weeks in his wife's company brought him no pleasure, either.

An hour later, he was fuming. It galled him that she put work on this herbal ahead of him. She was too "busy" to meet with him? When she was the one making demands of him to find out more about Lord Glenelg! The fact that he'd accomplished little in that direction did not lessen his ire at being left to cool his heels in the chamber Susanna had been sharing with Catherine.

The girl returned first. She looked no happier to see Robert than he was to be here. "Brother," she greeted him.

"I told you never to call me that."

"We are private here. No one lurks in the shadows, listening to your secrets."

"You are impertinent, Catherine. And in truth, my wife is lurking just behind you in the shadow of the door."

"I have a mind of mine own," the girl informed him.

"Aye, and I blame my wife for that."

"Why, thank you, my dear," Susanna said with a false smile as she came in behind the younger woman. "I am rather proud of Catherine's accomplishments, though I cannot take full credit for them."

"Catherine must move to the outer room and sleep on a pallet while I am here," he decreed.

Neither woman liked that pronouncement, but in this, at least, he had authority. "You have comfortable quarters, Susanna," he continued. "They will do well enough for us for the duration of my stay."

"Why have you come, Robert? I neither asked for nor expected your presence when I wrote to you of events here at Madderly Castle."

"You should never have written to me in such detail," he complained. "Much of what you committed to paper might have waited until I arrived."

"I did not know you would come," she repeated through clenched teeth.

"You might easily have contrived a way. Used a code or cipher."

"That seems a great deal of bother. Robert, why—"

"Would you rather have someone know you are investigating two murders? Alert them to the fact that I have come to help you?"

"Who would read my private letters to my husband? And who had opportunity? Each was sealed and sent on its way the same day I wrote it."

"There are many ways to intercept a missive ere it leaves the county. You are too trusting, wife."

Miffed, she fell silent, glaring at him.

"In future, you are always to use some cipher when you correspond with me."

"I know none."

"Nor do I," Catherine chimed in, "but I should like to learn. Is there some book that sets out instructions?"

"I have heard rumors," Susanna said, "that Giovanni Battista della Porta, the author of *Magic Naturalis*, is now working on one on cryptography."

There was a new note in her voice. Admiration. And Robert remembered how fascinated she'd been by della Porta's book on natural magic, in particular by his confutation of demonology.

"I fear you must submit to instruction at my hands," Robert told them, though he thought Catherine forward for including herself in the conversation and did not intend to teach her anything. "Before I leave Madderly Castle, I will make sure you learn all you need to know."

"I cannot begin to tell you how that news pleases me," Susanna said. "And it will please me even more to learn when you mean to depart."

"Not until I have completed my investigation of Lord Glenelg's murder."

"Your real reason for coming to Madderly Castle?"

"Aye."

"I was not told there had been a murder until after I arrived here."

"Pendennis saw no need to mention it."

"Was I sent for to work on an herbal, Robert, or to help you?"

"Your presence is merely the excuse for mine," he told her bluntly. "I am to discover why Glenelg was killed and who killed him."

"And Eleanor."

"And Eleanor," he agreed, though in truth he had no idea if the murders were connected or not. He supposed he must make some effort to placate Susanna. After all, it mattered not which one of them solved this crime. Credit would go to him.

Quickly and succinctly, leaving his wife no opening to ask questions, he summarized what he had learned of Lord Glenelg and his family in Scotland. Then he repeated all that Walter Pendennis had told him of treason and counterfeiting in Gloucestershire.

"Thus, learning the identity of Glenelg's killer is as important as catching him," he concluded. "We dare not assume that Glenelg's death brought to an end this threat to the Crown, though in fact it may have."

"So, it is possible an old enemy did kill Lord Glenelg," Susanna mused. Then, with as much clarity and preciseness as Robert himself had used in giving his account, she brought him up to date on her efforts to glean information since sending her second letter to him. She ended with Catherine's story about Sir Humphrey Radcliffe.

"Your memory served you well," Robert said. "It was Sir Humphrey who brought his daughter to court at the New Year. Mary is her name." He frowned. "I do not recall any mention of a half sister, but if she was estranged from her father, that is not surprising."

"Speaking of sisters, I am beginning to suspect Lord Madderly's sibling, Beatrice, knows more than she is saying, but since she will scarce speak two words together to me, and only then if they relate to the herbal, 'tis passing difficult to get answers from her."

"Shall I seduce her secrets out of her?" Robert asked.

"You have not met Beatrice yet, have you? She pled an

aching head and did not go to supper. She had food sent up to her in the workroom."

"That ugly?" Robert asked.

"Face like a horse."

"Some would say her bosom makes up for any lack," Catherine muttered. She blushed furiously when both Robert and Susanna turned to look at her.

Susanna regarded Catherine with a strangely jaundiced eye. "Your sister, Robert, has taken an uncommon interest in the doings of Gilbert Russell, Lord Madderly's gentleman usher. She seems to believe that he has lately been paying particular attention to Beatrice."

"I recall the comments about this fellow in your letter," Robert told her. "Is he not the one who accused you of Lady Madderly's murder? Mayhap he has now turned his suspicions on Beatrice."

He thought Susanna's agreement grudging. That she should suspect the lady was one thing. That her conclusion might agree with Master Russell's plainly annoyed her.

"Have either the bye-knife or your key turned up?" he asked her.

"Nay. I do think both must have been disposed of."

Robert was not so certain. There was one place they might have been hidden all this while. Lord Madderly's locked study both intrigued him and aroused his darkest suspicions.

Abruptly, he shifted his attention to Catherine. " 'Tis time you left us. I would have a private reunion with my wife." Susanna's discretion he trusted. Catherine was still an unknown entity. Giving them no opportunity to object, Robert crossed the bedchamber, threw open the door, and held it ajar until Catherine stalked through it.

"I keep no secrets from Catherine," Susanna told him in that haughty voice he hated.

"What if I sent her away so I could make love to you?" He closed and locked the door.

"Or beat me?" she inquired with false sweetness.

A sudden memory of guilty pleasure threw Robert off stride. The sharp set-down he had planned was never spoken. Instead he returned to the subject he wished to discuss with his wife.

"Lord Madderly is in the best position to plot against the queen, and he'd have had ample opportunity to kill Lord Glenelg."

"But why kill his own wife?"

"A man might have any number of reasons to want to do that."

"Aye. And a wife to kill her husband," she shot back, making him regret his taunt.

"I mean to search Lord Madderly's study at the first opportunity," he announced.

"It is always kept locked."

"That will not stop me, but the task will be easier if you distract him."

She sketched a mock curtsey. "Of course, my dear. I will do whatever you command. So glad to be of use to you."

"You have made little progress asking questions," he pointed out to her. "It is time for more forceful measures."

"On the contrary. I have gathered a great deal of information. What remains is to piece it together in the proper fashion. Now that I know what was previously kept from me, I have only to apply a logical mind to both questions and answers and the solution must inevitably follow."

"In the meantime, you live here in great comfort and will in time have produced another book on herbs. You have the easier part in this, Susanna."

"You will return to Edinburgh soon enough."

"Aye, but though the opportunities there to serve the queen are great, it is not an entirely pleasant post. Other cities are more fair. Even London. In Edinburgh solid blocks of tenements occupy the space between High Street and the Nor' Loch."

"Loch?"

"Lake. It is an artificial body of water originally designed to protect the city from the north. Now 'tis little more than an open sewer."

"And the tenements you mention?"

"Vile. Dwellings on the first floor are reached by rickety forestairs and inside they are dark and gloomy with naught but round holes cut in the rough-hewn boards for windows. A man can stick his head through to see what is happening outside, but little more."

She was looking at him strangely and he wondered if he was overdoing his attempt to make his living conditions seem unappealing. It had been Annabel's idea to deceive Susanna, lest she decide to join him in Scotland when the herbal was complete.

"The ground level of these tenements opens onto narrow alleys called wynds," he continued. Too late to change tactics now. "These wynds are filled with tar barrels, straw, broom, and wood, thus negating the effect of Edinburgh's ban on thatched roofs, a law intended to prevent fires."

"And this is the condition in Cowgate, too?" Susanna sounded skeptical.

"All parts of Edinburgh are crowded. And on the south side of High Street, where Cowgate lies, the worst of it is the smells. There are candlemakers near the Greyfriar's Port and maltmen around the West Port and the foot of Castle Hill. You know what a stench those trades produce. The only place in all of Edinburgh where one can go to breathe fresh air is an area called Greenside, the site of open-air performances of plays and of concerts by the town musicians. There one can sit upon the bank of the hill and pretend to be in England." He paused for effect. "Until the piping begins."

A grudging smile appeared on Susanna's face. However much she might doubt the rest of his account, she accepted that he despised the infernal screeching sounds made by that favorite Scots instrument, the bagpipe. After a moment, the smile widened, then was followed by a wry chuckle. Before long they were both laughing heartily.

This ability to see humor in the most unlikely places was the one thing they had always been able to share.

18

Catherine stormed out of the withdrawing room a short time after her eviction from the bedchamber, still incensed by her half brother's attitude. He'd dismissed her as if she were no more than a common servant!

Such treatment was typical of him. He thought nothing of his sister's feelings. For that matter, he cared little how his own wife felt. Catherine regarded Susanna as a martyr for her acceptance of that cruel fact.

When she wed, Catherine vowed, it would be no arranged marriage. She would choose her own husband, and he would be someone who cared for her. Someone who respected her opinions. Someone with whom she could form a partnership.

That was what Susanna claimed she had with Robert, but Catherine did much doubt it. Robert was too vain and self-centered to consider anyone his equal, least of all a woman.

Without conscious thought, Catherine headed toward the

stables. If Robert was here at Madderly Castle, then so was Vanguard. She might lack any rapport with the man, but she doted on his horse.

"Mistress Denholm!" The familiar voice greeted her as soon as she passed under the sprig of rowan nailed over the stable door to keep out witches. "Well met."

"Fulke!" She had forgotten he had accompanied Sir Robert to Scotland. Delighted to find an old friend from among the Leigh Abbey servants, especially one who shared her love of animals, Catherine so far forgot her present dignity as to throw herself into his arms and hug him tightly.

He was a strapping lad only a year or so older than she and returned her embrace with enthusiasm. Neither one of them gave a thought to how affectionate their greeting might appear to others until a loud throat-clearing sound interrupted their reunion. They sprang apart, suddenly all too aware of the difference in their stations and the misinterpretations that were possible. Catherine turned to find Gilbert Russell staring at her with disbelief and speculation in his eyes.

Resisting the urge to make excuses, she drew herself up straighter and glared. "Have you met mine old friend, Fulke, Master Russell?" she asked. "He was groom of the stable at Leigh Abbey when first I went to live there." She did not add that he had also been with Lady Appleton in Lancashire two years back and so knew much of what her early life had been like.

"A warm household at Leigh Abbey," Gilbert remarked.

"There's naught—"

Catherine cut short Fulke's red-faced defense by shoving him aside. With her left hand thrust out behind her to hold him back, she took a threatening step toward Gilbert and thumped him hard on the chest with her right fist. "I do not look down on servants as some people do," she declared. "And with Fulke I share a love of animals. What fault do you find with that?"

Recovering his aplomb, Gilbert offered a polite, apologetic bow. "Why, none at all, Mistress Denholm. What happens in the household at Leigh Abbey is none of my concern."

It was then she noticed that he wore a short, dark cloak, wrapped close around him against the night's chill. She glanced down to find high leather riding boots. He was going out on another of his nocturnal rambles. To meet a woman? Catherine suspected so. The possibility made her voice waspish.

"I came out to see Vanguard. What is your excuse?"

"The master's horse," Fulke put in. He was plainly ill at ease in this situation, but he would not leave her as long as Gilbert remained. Not unless Catherine ordered him to.

"I need no excuse," Gilbert mumbled.

His sudden uneasiness cheered her. "Come and meet him," Catherine invited. "He is a most splendid beast. Which stall is he in, Fulke?"

In solemn procession, the three of them filed along the planked floor past the stalls holding some thirty horses belonging to Madderly Castle. Most were the same golden dun color. Catherine stopped to greet her own dapple gray, Lady, and Susanna's roan, but they came at last to Vanguard.

Gilbert's attitude changed abruptly at the sight of him. Admiration for a fine piece of horseflesh vanquished his annoyance at encountering Catherine in the stable.

Men never seemed to care what a hunter looked like, she mused, so long as it had stamina enough for a day-long ride through open country or deer-park. Palfreys were only required to provide a comfortable snaffle-ride, in which the gait was never a trot or a gallop, always an amble, pace, or rack. But Vanguard was a courser, a horse of requisite "stately" appearance who displayed most of the traditional points of an ideal warhorse.

Catherine could almost hear Gilbert itemizing them as he ran one gloved hand over Vanguard's flank. Black hooves. Straight legs. Big knees. Sinewy thighs. Broad breast. Long, arched neck tapering toward the head. Small, sharp, upright ears. Large black eyes. Large mouth. A head shaped like that of a ram. A long thin mane. Full tail, reaching to the ground. General proportions, so Robert had once said, "like a stag," which meant the hindquarters were slightly lower than the forehand. To complete the perfection, Vanguard was all black except for a white blaze on his forehead.

"He is most excellent," Gilbert said.

"Which horse is yours?" Catherine asked. She signaled Fulke not to follow as Gilbert led the way back to the other end of the stable.

His courser was a big bay, broad backed and sturdy. What he lacked in stateliness, he made up for with a lively attitude. "Sprack as a banty-cock," Catherine muttered under her breath as Gilbert produced a curb bit and a military-style saddle with brass stirrups.

She talked to the horse as he was being readied to ride and only belatedly realized that Gilbert was looking at her strangely. "What?"

"I had not realized until I saw you with Sir Robert at supper that you were . . . related to the Appletons."

Catherine was uncertain how to respond. The truth was supposed to be kept secret, for her own protection. "Why should you think that I am?" she asked.

"You resemble Sir Robert a great deal."

"Oh. Well, I . . ." Her voice trailed off and she stared up at him in misery. She did not want to lie, but neither was she prepared to confide the whole sordid story. He might take a dislike to her if he knew she'd claimed the Denholm inheritance under false pretenses. Worse, he might feel that disqualified her as a prospective bride.

Not that he had given her any indication that he might offer for her, but she kept hoping he returned her interest. Sometimes he seemed to. When he wasn't showering his attention on Beatrice Madderly.

"Are you going to meet Beatrice somewhere?" she asked abruptly.

He stopped in the act of mounting. "Why would you think so?"

"Lady Appleton believes Beatrice has a lover." And Catherine herself had seen the woman hanging about the stables more than once, her manner furtive.

It was not the ideal place to make love, she reflected. Too many stable boys were in and out, and Edward and Philip, too. And Catherine herself. But if Gilbert rode out at night, might not Beatrice do the same and meet him in some rose-covered cottage and . . . let him bite her neck?

Hot color flooded into Catherine's face. Gilbert's sudden grin made her want to strike him.

"Why, Catherine. Are you jealous?"

She could feel the red hue deepen until her cheeks must have been bright as ripe cherries, but she refused to look away. "Merely curious," she declared.

His laughter was barely stifled. Insulted, Catherine drew herself up straighter and huffed. "You pay Beatrice much attention of late. Do not bother to deny it."

"She is my mistress."

"You admit it?"

"Mistress of this household, now that Lady Madderly is gone. Tell me, Catherine, how young are you?"

"What does my age have to do with anything?" She fought the urge to glance down at her bosom, so much smaller and less significant than the one Beatrice boasted.

"Nothing, I suppose. A maid may be ancient and still innocent."

"I am not innocent!" Not with everything that had happened in her past.

Abruptly Gilbert's smile turned into a frown. "We continue to speak at cross-purposes, or so I do hope."

"Is Beatrice a great heiress? I am."

Gilbert gave her an odd look, then began to lead his mount from the stable without answering her question. "I must go now, Catherine. Have that lad Fulke escort you back into the castle. Whatever you may think, you are far too untutored in the ways of the world to be abroad alone."

She followed him out into the night, more convinced than ever that he was going to meet Beatrice Madderly, even though she saw no sign of the noblewoman. Perhaps he just took the horse to disguise the fact that he did not have to travel far. Perhaps she could walk to their rendezvous.

But why ride out at all? The only reason she could conceive of was that he dared not risk being caught with Beatrice in her brother's house. Catherine thought it likely that Lord Madderly would disapprove of Gilbert as a suitor for his sister . . . for exactly the same reasons Robert would disapprove if Gilbert wanted her.

He had no title. He was not even a knight. He was a nobody. An upper servant.

More suited to herself than Beatrice.

After all, *Catherine* was not the daughter of a peer. And Gilbert was younger than Beatrice, though Catherine did not suppose that made much difference. She had heard of cases where very old ladies had married very young men. In fact, Susanna had told her of a most scandalous case just like that. The old duchess of Suffolk had married her groom of the stable after her first husband's death.

Lost in contemplation, Catherine did not at first understand what Gilbert meant when he spoke again.

"I suppose the resemblance between you became more plain as you grew older. It must have made things difficult, but it was good of Lady Appleton to befriend you. Her obvious affection for you must deter most gossips."

In slowly dawning horror, Catherine realized that Gilbert had jumped to an erroneous conclusion. He'd seen her with Robert, calculated their respective ages, and deduced that Robert was her father!

Irritation surfaced, but she bit back hasty words. That Gilbert should assume she was illegitimate was intolerable, yet the truth was every bit as unpalatable. He would think no more highly of her if he heard the real story of her birth and heritage.

She watched him mount in stony silence, perversely deciding not to correct him. Let him think what pleased him! 'Twas obvious to her now that he'd never had any true feelings for her, else he'd not have entertained such a possibility in the first place!

"I must not detain you longer," she said in a cold voice. "Doubtless you are bound on some urgent mission. There could be no other reason why such an upright soul as yourself would ride abroad in the dead of night."

He had the audacity to smile at her. " 'Tis scarce the dead of night. No more than an hour past evensong. And the moon makes the road near bright as day."

"Why do you ride out, then?" She hadn't meant to yield to curiosity again, but she could not seem to stop herself.

"This is the only time I have to myself." His voice gentled. "Do you never crave solitude, Catherine? A few hours to yourself, to think, to plan?"

Slowly, she nodded. She could understand that need very well. But did he tell her true? A stubborn spark of hope flared deep in her heart. Mayhap he was not meeting anyone, after all.

Someday, she decided as she watched him ride out of sight, she would tell him the truth about herself. 'Twas likely the only certain way to gauge the measure of the man.

19

While all the rest of the household was attending Sunday services in the chapel at Madderly Castle the next day, Robert broke into Lord Madderly's study, searched it thoroughly, then returned to his wife's bedchamber.

Susanna entered the room in a rush, eager to hear his report, a few minutes after his own arrival. Her prayer book landed on the table with a thump. "Well?"

"No apparent treason," he said, but he had difficulty containing his amusement.

Susanna's brows arched. "What, then, is he hiding?"

"An extensive and enlightening collection of what are popularly called Lucretias." The tabletop-sized portraits all had frames of gilded wood and he'd found most of them wrapped in velvet and stored in a purpose-made box decorated with a scene of the Annunciation. Each had a metal ring attached, as did the one Madderly had suspended for easy viewing from his desk.

"Oh." Eyes widening, Susanna attempted to absorb this news without laughing. She did not succeed. The thought of Lord Madderly surrounding himself with paintings of naked women was too much for her. She collapsed next to Robert on the bed and all but whooped with it, sparking his own mirth once more. A good ten minutes passed before they could calm themselves enough to discuss their next move in anything resembling a rational manner.

Susanna was the first to recover. "Were we wrong, then, to suspect Lord Madderly of complicity in a treasonous conspiracy?"

"It is too soon to exonerate him. Someone in these parts is counterfeiting seals in order to lend authenticity to forged papers. Madderly would not be doing the work himself. If he is involved, he is the mastermind behind the plan. All I can say for certain is that I found no evidence of treason in his study."

"*Nothing* suspicious besides the Lucretias? I do not see why he'd trouble to keep the room locked for those. He takes no such precautions to hide books with . . . lively illustrations."

"You have not seen these particular paintings." And would not, Robert decided. Susanna had too much intellectual curiosity as it was. "There is another entrance to the study," he told her. "A concealed door. But such things are not uncommon in a castle. Once upon a time, escape routes were highly prized during sieges."

Distracted, as he'd hoped she would be, Susanna demanded details. "Where does it lead?"

"Into the thickness of the wall. The exit is on the outside

on the level below. A narrow, winding stair. To judge by the cobwebs, it has not been much used of late."

"Glenelg's killer might have left that way. That murder was weeks ago."

"A quarrel among thieves? Madderly killed him, then crept away?" Something about the theory did not ring true, but Robert could not put his finger on the flaw in the logic.

"Does the queen have any reason besides proximity to the counterfeiting to suspect Lord Madderly of treason?" Susanna asked.

"She may regard him with a jaundiced eye because he rarely comes to court." Being ignored always affronted Queen Elizabeth. "And Pendennis observed that it is expensive to collect things." He'd made the remark while examining Robert's possessions in Edinburgh. "How is it that Lord Madderly can afford so many books?"

They had remained on the bed, facing each other. Now Susanna sat up, plumped the down pillows, and tucked two behind her for support, prepared to give this matter of treason her full attention. "What you say makes sense. Lord Madderly may be involved. But who else? 'Tis unlikely he's creating the forgeries himself."

Robert flopped over onto his back and stared at the green velvet canopy overhead. "A craftsman with the skill to copy the intricate designs used on seals and signet rings might come from any walk of life."

"Man or woman?"

"Aye," Robert reluctantly conceded.

"So, Lady Madderly might have been in charge, until she died. Perhaps, like Lord Glenelg, she angered a fellow conspirator."

"More likely she discovered something she should not have." He ran agitated fingers through his hair. "I tell you true, Susanna. I like not these mysteries. We cannot even be sure Glenelg died because he was involved in the conspiracy. 'Tis speculation only."

"Sensible speculation. And if Eleanor could have been involved, so could Magdalen Harleigh and Beatrice Madderly."

"I leave the women to you."

Suddenly Susanna's face appeared above his, her expression rueful as she began to toy with the laces holding his small face ruff in place. "Beatrice is too full of resentment to cooperate with me. For some reason she covets the job of supervising the completion of the herbal. She was taken by surprise when her brother asked me to stay and her disapproval is plain for all to see."

"Catherine tells me you think Beatrice has a lover."

He'd managed to startle her. She sat up, tucking her legs beneath her tailor-fashion, and gave him a hard look. "When did she say that to you?"

"We had a brief discussion this morning." He'd awakened early and gone out to reconnoiter the castle. He'd all but tripped over Catherine's pallet in the outer chamber and she'd responded by getting up, getting dressed, and following him.

Susanna looked worried, as well she should. Her chick was getting ready to leave the nest. "Did you approach Catherine or did she approach you? She's never been all that fond of you, Robert."

"And well I know it, dear wife. I owe that, in part, to you." When she started to object, he placed a finger against her lips to stay her words. "Hear me out. She told me more of Beatrice, but of greater import is an unanticipated problem of a personal nature."

"What problem?"

One better discussed in an upright position, Robert decided. He swung his legs over the side of the bed and stood. "In the two years since we discovered the truth about Catherine, she has grown ever more like an Appleton in her coloring and features. I know not how many others have noticed the similarities, but Master Russell was not deceived for one moment. He knew at once that Catherine had Appleton blood in her veins. Catherine says he thinks she is mine."

"Yours?" Susanna looked blank. Then comprehension dawned and anger flashed in her eyes as she bounded from the bed. "How dare he!"

"You thought the same yourself once."

"Robert, this is serious. What if he says something? Catherine could become the object of malicious gossip."

"Catherine? Catherine's reputation is the least of our worries!" Robert knew he sounded short-tempered, but he was the one who would suffer most if gossip reached those with influence at court. "I could be accused of fraud for urging Catherine to claim the Denholm estate."

"Nonsense. Not when Randall Denholm had the good sense to leave a will making Catherine his heir. There is no question but that the inheritance is hers."

"There would be scandal. We do not want that."

"No," Susanna agreed, "we do not want that. Did Catherine admit anything to Master Russell?"

"She says not, but neither did she deny his suspicion."

"What would it profit her to let him think she is your daughter?"

"Who knows the reasoning women use?"

Hands curled into fists at her sides, Susanna glared at him. "Catherine is an uncommon sensible young woman. He must have hurt her feelings in some way."

"She is jealous of Beatrice Madderly." Any fool could see that, though why she should think Beatrice was any competition, Robert could not fathom.

"Back to Beatrice." Susanna looked thoughtful, always a dangerous sign. "Go you and talk to her, Robert. She must know more than she's said. She runs this place for her brother, and did so even when Eleanor was alive."

He conjured up an image from the one brief glimpse he'd so far gotten of Beatrice Madderly. There were compensations. Beatrice's spectacular bosom came to mind. Robert looked at his wife and managed a wry smile. "Any sacrifice for you, my love."

20

Gilbert Russell watched with considerable amusement as Sir Robert Appleton sat down next to Beatrice Madderly on a high-backed bench. The courtier was a bit obvious in his admiration of the dog and lion finials and linenfold panels that decorated this piece of oak and walnut furniture. Beatrice, however, did not seem to think his conversation odd, nor was she inclined to send Sir Robert away.

Since Gilbert had recently tried similar ploys in an effort to discover Beatrice's secrets, and been obliged to endure an hour's meaningless chatter about the linnet she kept in a cage and her fear that Master Wheelwright's ferret would get loose one day and eat the bird, he wished the other man joy of her.

And luck.

Beatrice might well know something about Lord Glenelg's murder. Her whereabouts were unknown during the crucial period when the Scots baron had been killed. Had she returned to the library and seen something she shouldn't? Or had she been the one who stabbed Glenelg? He wouldn't put murder past her. She had a mean streak.

Catherine came up beside him, distracting him. "A pity Beatrice is so fickle," she remarked.

"Think you so?" Catherine's jealousy alternately amused and alarmed Gilbert. She was growing much too attached to him.

And he continued to find her far more attractive than he wanted to. For his own peace of mind, this dangerous flirtation could not continue. There were too many things she did not know about him, things he could not tell her without making matters even more difficult.

"I have as goodly an inheritance," she informed him.

"So you said before. Do you think money the only thing that motivates a man?" He felt a genuine curiosity to hear her answer.

Catherine pretended an interest in the ceiling, an expanse of red pine thinly coated with grasso and then painted. It was decorated with interlacing stems bearing leaves and fruits. Slowly she shifted her gaze to the frieze at the bottom, which showed hunting scenes and coats of arms. The families of both Lord Madderly's wives had been included with his own.

"What else would?" she finally asked.

He realized he'd almost forgotten the question.

What motivated a man when it came to finding a woman to marry? He spoke before he took time to think his answer through. "Politics."

"Not the response I was expecting." Catherine ran a finger around the rim of an Italian majolica vase that had been placed on a nearby table, as if she was considering carefully what she would say to him next.

"Did you think I would say love?" he asked.

"I never know what you will say!" Abruptly abandoning the vase, she started to walk away. He caught her arm and tugged, pulling her in close to his side.

"I have angered you." Again. In spite of his earlier resolve, he eased her nearer still, until she was almost touching him from breast to knees.

She had no choice but to tilt her head back and meet his steady gaze. "You can be most unkind." She did not flinch when she said the words. He admired her for that.

" 'Twas not my intention, Catherine. I would be very kind to you indeed, if matters were different."

"What matters? I—"

"Murder," he cut in. "There are two murders standing between us, sweeting."

"You cannot still believe Lady Appleton killed Lady Madderly."

"Likely not."

For a moment, she fumed silently at his refusal to exonerate her friend. Then she struck back. "She will discover who killed both Lord Glenelg and Lady Madderly and bring him to justice. You will see. She is the cleverest woman in all Christendom."

"Women should not meddle in such matters. Think of the danger."

"I laugh at danger!" Eyes flashing, she was beautiful to behold, but he began now to grow seriously alarmed. Such boldness could lead her into worse trouble than she knew.

"Be wary, lass." He tightened his grip on her arms. "Think

on this. Lady Madderly died because she was a threat to someone, no doubt the same someone who killed Lord Glenelg. This killer acts on impulse, using the first weapon that comes to hand. He turned Glenelg's own knife upon him. That added to the thrill. The next time it was even easier. He seized up a candlestick. A third murder would not trouble such a fiend at all. 'Twould be the work of a moment."

Another woman might have fainted dead away. Or at least turned pale. Catherine glared at him. "If you believe that, why did you not speak up and tell Lord Madderly so? He continues to advance the foolish theory that there were two separate intruders and that the rest of us have naught to fear."

"Mayhap I am the killer," Gilbert suggested in a low voice.

Catherine gave a snort of disbelief. "You have no motive. Lady Appleton says no one kills without a reason."

"Lady Appleton does not dismiss her suspicions of me so lightly," he reminded her.

"She does not know you as I do."

"Do you know me as well as you think? Be careful, Catherine. Be very careful."

The urge to protect her from her own folly was distressingly strong. He wanted to keep her here in his arms forever, where she would be safe.

Safe? Gilbert marveled at his own skill at self-deception. She would not be safe with him. His very feelings for her placed her in danger.

The words that would drive her away were on his lips, but he never had the chance to utter them. Lady Appleton forestalled him.

"There you are, Catherine," she said in that peremptory

tone that suggested barely suppressed anger. "Come along, child. We have work to do on the herbal today."

She ignored Gilbert.

He returned the favor.

But he could not help watching until they left the room. Just before she walked through the door, Catherine looked back and smiled wistfully at him.

Two emotions shone clearly in her eyes, impossible for him to mistake. The first was love. That was a burden in itself. But the trust he also saw in her gaze was even harder for him to deal with. The message she sent with just a look would have made a stronger man than Gilbert Russell quake in his boots.

21

Why not take Catherine with us," Susanna demanded.

"She will slow us down. If you are so concerned about her, then stay here yourself. I will journey to Elnestow alone."

"Since the excuse we have given for leaving is a visit to my sick uncle in Oxford, I fear that might arouse suspicion."

Would this trip yield any information they could use? she wondered as she folded clothing to pack in her capcase. Or were they beginning to clutch at straws?

"Why are you so worried about Catherine?" Robert lounged on the window seat, no help at all in the preparations for this trip.

"She is infatuated with Gilbert Russell. She seeks his company at every opportunity. It does not seem wise to leave her unchaperoned."

"Ask Magdalen Harleigh to keep an eye on the girl."

"If Catherine believes she is advancing our investigation," Susanna said slowly, "she will be more biddable." She had only to find a safe task for her to perform, something to keep her too busy to spend much time with Gilbert. "The school-room," she murmured.

"What about it?" Robert asked.

"I will ask Catherine to increase the time she spends in the schoolroom, on the pretext of observing Master Wheel-wright. I will tell her we need to eliminate suspects and that he, and Lord Madderly's sons for that matter, must be ruled out."

Robert looked up from the all-absorbing task of smoothing the pleats in his doublet. " 'Tis possible she may even learn something useful. Boys often observe what others miss and I warrant they will talk to a pretty girl."

"They are young yet for an interest in females," Susanna said, but it was with a lighter heart that she finished packing for their trip.

Less than an hour later, after brief private conversations with both Catherine and Magdalen, Susanna was waiting by the gatehouse for her horse to be brought out.

"No harm will come to me here while you are gone," Catherine blithely insisted. "If naught else, I have Master Russell to protect me."

"And who is to protect him from you?"

Catherine blushed. Susanna frowned.

"I will look out for both of them," Magdalen promised. She lowered her voice to add, "I will keep her too busy to dog Gilbert's footsteps. Not that there's any harm in him."

"I wish I could be certain of that."

Magdalen sighed. "Can we be sure of anything? Still, you need not fear for young Catherine. Beatrice has ordered preparations for Yuletide to begin. Even though we are a house in mourning, some traditions must be observed. The village folk have a right to expect entertainment."

"What task have you in mind for Catherine?"

"Making conserves, I do think. We will open a barrel of quinces and make codinac."

Susanna nodded her approval. Codinac was a combination of codlings and quinces and one of her personal favorites. And in the kitchen, Catherine would be as far out of Gilbert Russell's path as she would be in the schoolroom. Gilbert, Susanna had noticed, did not seem to care for Master Wheelwright. Or his ferret.

"She could do worse," Robert remarked as they rode southeast toward Burford. Lake and fen alike were frostbound, but Susanna could see by the silvery glint of the nearby trout stream that it was as yet unfrozen. "Master Russell would have to marry her, of course, but—"

"Do not be absurd! He is a nobody. No fortune. No position." And too much like Robert at his most charming for Susanna's peace of mind. She wanted better for Catherine.

"Are you certain he has no useful family connections?"

"Catherine asked him. He admitted to being but the landless third son of an obscure Warwickshire family."

"Where in Warwickshire?"

"Stratford-upon-Avon."

"Shall we stop there on our way back from Bedfordshire? It is but a day's journey out of our way and the delay might be worthwhile."

Susanna chided herself for not thinking of it first. If they were going to travel such a long way to reassure themselves that Eleanor's background was what she'd claimed, then most assuredly they must make the same inquiries into Gilbert Russell's antecedents.

The Cotswolds villages through which they passed, tiny places with stone buildings of simple construction, were for the most part tucked into little valleys. A pattern of stone walls divided field from field in place of hedgerows. The hilly tracks, Susanna learned, were called pitches when they made their way down the banks.

Everywhere they rode, sheep grazed, long-necked creatures with stocky bodies and broad buttocks. It was no wonder, she thought, that the folk in these parts derived most of their income from wool. The fleece on these beasts was deep and thick and even their foreheads were tufted with useable amounts.

Susanna shivered as another gust eddied beneath her cloak, envying the thick coat that kept the sheep warm. The wind had an edge.

At last the land began to slope gradually downward, descending into the valley of the Thames. The air was warmer, but the roads were no better. English roads were notoriously bad everywhere and particularly dangerous at this time of year, when frost glazed over the deepest ruts, disguising them until it was too late to avoid them. They had many mishaps, but no one was injured and the horses escaped without a single broken leg.

During the long trek across Oxfordshire and Buckinghamshire to Bedfordshire, Susanna had time to think. Too much time. Long before they'd reached the university city of

Oxford, she'd realized that Robert, as usual, was keeping something from her.

Resentment began to simmer beneath a calm exterior. It would do no good to demand answers, but if she bided her time she might coax them out of him. Unfortunately, patience had never been her strong suit.

"Did you know I would be used in this way before you left Leigh Abbey?" she asked as they set out from Oxford on yet another cold, crisp morning.

He gave her a hurt look. "How could I?"

"That is what I want to know, Robert. How could you?"

"You give me too much credit. This scheme was the queen's own, Susanna, and none of mine. I'd rather have stayed in Edinburgh."

She frowned at that slip of the tongue. Well, she'd known his complaints about Scotland had been exaggerated for effect. She'd not lower herself to ask about his diplomatic mission . . . or his amusements, either.

Although apparently unaware of her thoughts, Robert chose this moment to introduce a topic sure to distract her. "I am thinking that this journey provides me with an opportunity to expand your education," he said. " 'Tis time you learned to use codes and ciphers."

The steady plodding of their horses along the beaten path underscored his words. Ahead rode Fulke, their own trusted groom. He was armed, as was Robert. Behind them came a party of four men and their servants, with whom they'd joined for the safety in numbers along the road.

"Codes and ciphers," Susanna repeated as genuine curiosity fueled her interest. Temporarily, she forgot her annoyance at Robert. "What is the difference between the two?"

"Codes are impossible to read without some sort of key-code book. Words or phrases are represented by predetermined words, numbers, or symbols. Ciphers transpose the letters of plain text, or substitute other letters or symbols for the originals in the message. In some cases, we use a combination of methods according to a prearranged system."

"Is that not confusing?"

"That is the point of it," Robert reminded her. "To further confuse the enemy, all codes and ciphers in use are frequently changed. If they are repeated too often, they will be broken."

"But if only two people have the key, and something happens to them, then a message might never be read, even by those it most concerns."

"The queen employs experts to decode messages her agents intercept. 'Twould take time, but nothing is indecipherable."

Susanna wondered if he saw the contradiction in his claims, but decided not to point it out to him. If he believed his codes unbreakable by the enemy, so be it.

"One simple code involves substitution," he continued as the horses moved slowly over the uneven terrain. "For an *a*, you skip from the first letter of the alphabet to the fourth and write a *d*. For a *b*, use *e*, and so on to compose your message. A more complex variation is to place the coded letters so that they spell out a message only when read down one side of the page. The first letter of each line, for example, is the only one the person who receives the letter needs to look at."

"And must the content of the whole letter also make sense?"

He shrugged. "That is not necessary. If someone has intercepted the message he no doubt already knows it has a hidden meaning."

An argument, she thought, for writing in plain English. Not one of these suspicious intelligence gatherers would ever believe a missive meant precisely what it said.

"There are also all manner of numerical and hieroglyphic codes," Robert continued. "Usually they include nullities, which are meaningless ciphers designed to confuse."

She smiled at that notion and said mildly, "I would prefer something simple, but I suspect your preference runs to complexity."

These intelligence gatherers were naught but overgrown boys playing games. And they appeared to relish the search for conspiracies. Susanna wondered if they invented them if none were to be found. It would not surprise her in the least to learn they did.

"You might also make up your code merchant-wise," Robert suggested.

"And how is that, pray?"

"Use trading and business terms with prearranged meanings. What might seem to others to be a list of things you wish me to purchase for you in Edinburgh would actually be an account of your latest discoveries about Lord Glenelg's activities at Madderly Castle."

"This cryptography is a vexing business," Susanna muttered. "I like not so much secrecy. I had thought our nation was at peace at last."

"If it is to remain so, certain measures remain necessary. As to codes between us, perhaps there is a simpler method than shopping lists. Before I return to Edinburgh, we will decide upon a book. Your herbal, perhaps. Our code will then consist of a series of numbers for each word. You write the page number, the number of the line, and how many words in from the margin the chosen word lies."

This still sounded like a great deal of work to Susanna, and she remained unconvinced of the need for it, but she'd thought of an alternate volume to suggest. "Let us use Master John Knox's book," she suggested, struggling to keep a straight face. "I believe it is called *The First Blast of the Trumpet Against the Monstrous Regiment of Women.*"

"*You* have a copy?" He sounded astonished, then caught sight of the twinkle in her eyes and laughed.

"Lord Madderly does have one in his library." She smiled sweetly at him. "And I am sure you can obtain one in Edinburgh . . . if you have not done so already."

"We will use your herbal," he said in a firm voice.

They rode on in considerably more charity with each other.

22

Elnestow was a small place. It did not take long to discover what Robert had already begun to suspect. Eleanor had lied about her parentage. Sir Humphrey Radcliffe had never been married before he wed the beauteous Isabelle. And if he had sired Eleanor at all, then he had been a most precocious child.

Neither Sir Humphrey nor any of his family were at home, having traveled to London in order to spend the Yuletide season near daughter Mary at court. Of those Robert questioned, even those he bribed, none knew of a woman of nearly forty years of age, with Eleanor's description, who might have come from the area.

They started back toward Gloucestershire the following morning, again traveling with a party of merchants for safety. It was not an unpleasant journey. They stopped to visit friends along the way, spending a night at an inn when they were too far from any acquaintance's house to bespeak hospitality. When they reached Stratford-upon-Avon they had several comfortable inns to choose from and selected the Swan. Robert settled Susanna in the best chamber and went off alone. He returned several hours later in good spirits, having spent eightpence to have his hair and beard washed and trimmed and considerably more at a nameless tavern in Middle Row, another in High Street, and finally a third called the King's House in Rother Market.

"There is no family named Russell here with three sons," he announced to his wife. "And Master Russell's description yielded no other name."

"So I was told, too."

"By whom?" Robert blinked at her, realizing he was more bleary-eyed from the ale he'd consumed than he'd realized.

"By mine host, Master Dixon, and his wife. And also by the schoolmaster, one William Smart. He was a fellow at Christ's College, Cambridge, and knew of my father's work on languages there. Smart has been schoolmaster here for seven years and so would surely know if any local men went to work at Madderly Castle. The surname Russell is not that common and even of Gilberts there are but few. There is a Gilbert Bradley, who is a glover in Henley Street, but Master Smart knew no other by that name."

Refreshed by her own ablutions with a twopenny sponge, Susanna had set her mind to work, considering possibilities. She was a tiring woman to live with.

" 'Tis hardly a surprise to discover this deception after what we found in Elnestow," she said.

"You think the lies are connected?"

"It is the strangest coincidence otherwise, that two people

who live in Madderly Castle have lied about their families, their background."

"At best Eleanor Madderly was born a bastard," Robert agreed. "At worse, she was a complete imposter with no connection to the Radcliffe family at all."

"Do you think Lord Madderly knows the truth about his wife?"

"Does any man?" he muttered.

"I hope Catherine is safe," Susanna murmured, ignoring him. "We seem to have wasted our time on this journey. We might have been better employed seeking information where we were."

"On the contrary. We now know both Eleanor Madderly and Gilbert Russell for liars. At the same time, we have allayed suspicion about our reasons for being at Madderly Castle by leaving."

"We might have sent a servant to ask questions."

"He would have learned nothing, even with a letter to Sir Humphrey from you or me. Our questions would have been deemed impertinent and ignored."

"And Gilbert? Is he the killer? We left Catherine with him, Robert. I cannot—"

"Shhh!"

To Robert's surprise, she fell silent obediently, allowing him to verify that the faint sounds he'd been hearing for the last few minutes had also abruptly ceased.

Robert signaled her to remain quiet. He felt taut as a bowstring as he drew his dagger and cautiously approached the door. Someone was out there and he sensed more than a curious servant. His heart pumping courage, Robert flung open the portal and charged into the corridor.

The first man was armed with a crabtree cudgel, the second with a cowlstaff. "Pash him," the villain cried as soon as Robert appeared.

Out of the corner of his eye, Robert saw Susanna follow him, carrying the closest thing to a weapon she could find. The chamber pot was pewter. It connected with the second attacker's head with a resounding thump, but failed to render him unconscious. With a bellow, he turned on her. Susanna wisely screamed for help.

The next few minutes were filled with confusion, but the commotion soon brought the innkeeper and, from the stableyard below, Fulke and several other stalwart lads. One moment Robert was held at bay by two menacing strangers, the next they'd turned and fled, but not before the one with the cudgel had landed a blow on Robert's shoulder powerful enough to send him spinning into the wall.

"Go after them!" Susanna shouted to the rescue party.

She was obeyed, but too slowly. Even as Robert groaned and tried to sit up, the first report came back.

"Got the ballow," a stable boy announced, holding up the cudgel. The malefactor who'd wielded it had gotten clean away.

"Do not try to stand," Susanna warned. "You are bleeding from a cut on the head."

"My shoulder sustained greater damage." He winced as he tried to lift his arm.

"Help me get him into the bedchamber," Susanna ordered Fulke.

By the time he'd been undressed and propped up in bed, Susanna had commissioned Philippa, the innkeeper's wife, to fetch healing herbs and clean cloths and other necessities for his treatment. Robert found he was torn between making the most of his minor injuries to elicit sympathy and going out into the town in search of his assailants.

"Stay still," Susanna muttered as, for the second time, she applied plasters she had made for the pain and swelling. "I'd have preferred herb twopence stamped and boiled in olive oil, with some rosin, wax, and turpentine added thereto, but one does the best one can."

"What are you using?" he asked.

"First a decoction of self-heal, wine, and water." She removed the plaster from the back of his head and proceeded to anoint the injury with a substance whose stickiness offended him, especially on his clean hair.

Reaching back, he touched it, then brought the finger to his nose. "Honey?" He tasted. Honey.

"Honey," she agreed. "Followed by regular applications of a plaster made of rye meal, white of eggs, and juice of serpent's tongue, which hereabout is known as waybread."

"My head aches," he complained.

"Drink this."

"What is it?"

"Rosemary steeped in white wine."

The wine sounded promising, so he complied.

"Later I will lay self-heal bruised with oil of roses and vinegar to your forehead. That will soothe away any pain that remains, but rest will help most of all."

"How can I rest when someone has just tried to kill me?"

"Perhaps the attack was simply an attempt at robbery."

"No. They meant to kill me."

"You know who sent those men?"

"No, but I have many enemies."

"You are quick to think yourself the only one in danger. Why do you assume no one is after me? We have both been asking questions about the murders."

She was an annoying woman. Especially when she made a valid point. "Those at Madderly Castle believe we are in Oxford," he reminded her.

"Someone could have followed us."

"Why should they be suspicious? Unless Catherine revealed our true destination." With his head banging away, he made no effort at tact. "Aye. Likely she told Gilbert Russell."

Susanna was limping slightly as she moved from bed to table, putting away her herbs and potions. 'Twas an old injury, now aggravated by the long days on horseback in cold weather. "Catherine would not betray us," she insisted. "She knew our mission must be carried out in secret."

"Can you be certain? And Gilbert is the one who creeps out of the castle at night. He'd find it easy enough to send word ahead to some villain, ordering him to follow us, to stop us before we learned anything significant."

"This is all speculation. It rests on the assumption that what we have learned on this journey is important in some way, but as yet there is no link between Eleanor's lies and those told by Gilbert, and neither is directly linked to Glenelg's murder."

"I cannot accept the coincidence of two separate murderers in Madderly Castle."

"Aye. I grant you that is far-fetched." She paused as if struck by a thought. "The only connection seems to be Lord Madderly."

"You think he is the killer?" Robert's interest quickened.

He could almost forget his aching head while they strove to put the pieces of the puzzle together.

Susanna perched on the end of his bed. "I do not know if he is or not. But what if he did not know Eleanor lied? What if, in order to be worthy to marry a baron of the realm, she forged documents to show her descent from the earls of Sussex?"

"A counterfeit genealogy? How could she dare hope she'd not be found out?"

"She dared and she succeeded. No one else questioned her background until we came along. As to whether she told Lord Madderly the truth after they were wed, he must answer that question. Mayhap she simply convinced him that the rift with her family was so great that they'd not care to hear her spoken of. It might have worked. How often would Lord Madderly come in contact with Sir Humphrey or the present earl of Sussex? 'Tis well known he does not care for life at court. Eleanor may have believed herself safe from discovery."

"But what point to convincing a prospective husband of her background if she could not bring a dowry from that source? Surely he must have dealt with her father before they wed."

"They were both of mature years. Perhaps she only needed to convince him she was wellborn, that she was worthy to be a baron's wife by virtue of her noble father's birth."

"And her real parentage?"

"Yeoman stock?" Susanna suggested.

That did seem likely. Robert nodded, a movement that reminded him, painfully, of his broken head.

"Lowborn she might have been," Susanna mused, "but if so I can only admire Eleanor the more. She rose above her circumstances. Had she lived, she'd have earned praise for her work on the herbal, once I'd corrected her mistakes."

"She lied and cheated." Robert spoke through teeth clenched against renewed throbbing.

Susanna gave him a pointed look, but did not say aloud that he did the same. After studying his expression a moment longer, she hopped off the bed and went to fetch the soothing compress she had promised him.

The question they should be asking, Robert thought as he watched her quick, efficient preparations, was how Lady Madderly's actions tied her to a treasonous conspiracy.

23

Catherine abandoned her stool in favor of a pile of cushions near the fire as soon as the servants began to dismantle the parlor table after supper, but she took with her a bowl of dried fruit. She was nibbling a date when Gilbert sat down beside her.

"Are you fond of those?" He took one for himself. "Cook uses stoned dates to prepare a sweet *Leche Lumbarde.*"

"I do like dates, and raisins, too, but does not *Leche Lumbarde* require kneading ginger into the dates? I do not care for ginger." If she remembered aright, *Leche Lumbarde* was also served with a syrup made of sweetened red wine, another thing she did most dislike.

"Marchpane, then?" Gilbert persisted. "There's no ginger in marchpane."

"Naught but blanched almonds, sugar, and rosewater," Catherine agreed. "Lady Appleton has her cook ice march-

177

pane with colored sugar." Just a pinch of sandalwood turned it pink; saffron produced yellow in shades from pale primrose to marigold.

Though her conversation with Gilbert was far from intimate, for all that he kept dipping his fingers into her bowl of dried fruit, Catherine was not surprised when Magdalen joined them, placing her cushion between them and obliging Gilbert to give way. She did not need to be so obvious, Catherine thought resentfully, but Gilbert flashed her a mischievous grin and at once she felt less put-upon.

It had taken her but a day to realize Susanna was trying to keep her too busy to spend any time alone with Gilbert. The quest for answers in the schoolroom was a rude ploy. Magdalen's watchdog role was even less subtle.

Resigned, Catherine had decided to cooperate in her own protection. She enjoyed her visits with the boys and their master of grammar. For fun, she'd been flirting with Master Wheelwright, letting him think he was the reason she'd volunteered to help tutor Latin and Greek and wanted to learn how to carve.

Evenings were congenial, spent here in the parlor before the fire. Lord Madderly and his sister supped in solitary splendor in the great chamber and went early to bed, leaving the upper servants to their own devices. Sometimes they played card games or chess. Or Magdalen strummed her lute and they sang part songs. This evening, though, both Otto Harleigh and Master Borden, the steward, claimed they had business to attend to elsewhere. They'd left at the same time the servants carried off the damask tablecloth and napkins. Those who remained were content to warm themselves by the hearth and discuss plans for the Yuletide celebrations.

"There will be lamprey pie," the chaplain told Catherine. A most secular longing came into his eyes at the thought of crusts shaped in special wooden molds. "And snails served with onions and pepper and dressed with strong vinegar."

"Does brawn appear hereabout as a holiday dish?" Catherine asked.

"Lady Madderly mentioned it once," Magdalen recalled, "but I know not how to prepare it."

Master Wheelwright spoke before Catherine could. "Brawn is the forepart of a tame boar," he explained. "In Lancashire, in rich gentlemen's houses, the beast is fed on oats and peas for a year or more and lodged on the bare planks of an uneasy cote till his fat be hardened sufficiently for the purpose. Some are slaughtered in the autumn, but most are saved for Christmas. The neck pieces are called collars of brawn, the shoulders shields."

Catherine took up the account when it moved from slaughterhouse to kitchen.

"Each piece is wrapped with bulrushes and then boiled in a great cauldron until the meat is so tender that one may thrust a soft straw clean through the fat. After the pieces cool, they are put into close vessels and over them are poured either good small ale or beer mingled with verjuice and salt. So covered, the soused brawn is left until it is time to serve it. 'Tis said to be best with a draught of malmsey, bastard, or muscatel drunk after it."

"What is done with the other parts of the boar?" Magdalen wanted to know.

"The hinder parts being cut off, they are first drawn with lard and then boiled, then soused in claret wine and vinegar and afterward baked in pasties and eaten. Brawn and mustard is a great favorite for breakfast, too."

"The equivalent favorite here is Tewkesbury ham," Magdalen told her. "It is pickled first and then smoked in peat for at least two months."

"Is it ready now to bake?"

"Not until we've soaked it in water for twelve hours."

"You make me hungry just listening," Gilbert said. "And that after all these dates and raisins." Catherine looked into her bowl, surprised to find it empty.

"How go the plans for entertainment?" Magdalen asked him.

"Will there be mumming?" Catherine interrupted before he could answer. She could not imagine Christmas and Twelfth Night without mummers, but this was not Lancashire, or even Kent.

"That and gambling," Gilbert promised. "Lord Madderly wishes the holidays to proceed as they always have. The black hangings are to be removed everywhere but in his bedchamber, where he will keep him to himself instead of presiding over the hall."

"That duty falls to the King of the Bean in any event," Magdalen reminded him.

"Is the King of the Bean the same as a Lord of Misrule?" Catherine thought he must be, a mock prince chosen to preside over all eating and drinking from Christmas Eve through Twelfth Night.

"Aye," Gilbert said. "And this year the fellow who found

the bean in his portion of cake is Ralph, one of the gardeners, a burly fellow with a roar like a lion and a laugh that can crack windows. He has by now named a Fool and a Jester as his two chief assistants. All will meet them on the morrow, for I'm told it is the custom hereabout for them to enter the chapel just after services."

The next day, glad of Gilbert at her side to protect her, Catherine watched as some twenty lusty lads burst into the sanctuary. A half dozen of them carried their "king" on a litter while others rode wooden hobby horses. On King Ralph's head was a tinsel crown. He wore a robe of yellow green together with gaudy scarves and ribbons and as many rings as he could fit on his fingers. Small bells had been tied to his legs and to the legs of all his entourage. Their tinkling sound was the least of the noise. Pipes and drums and pots and pans added to the cacophony.

Only at the very foot of the chancel did they stop their onslaught, making a mock obeisance to the chaplain before they started back down the side aisles.

"There will be dancing now," Gilbert whispered in Catherine's ear as the marauders left. "All are welcome to join in."

"Out-of-doors?"

"Why not? The day is a fine one." He grinned. "Why, they tell me that in these parts, nine years out of ten, autumn lingers into the new year and Christmas Day itself is still so warm as to be almost springlike."

This was the second time in two days that Gilbert had made remarks to distance himself from Gloucestershire ways. "Is Warwickshire so different?" Catherine wondered aloud.

That county was, after all, not many miles away to the east, and still part of the Cotswolds, too.

It was a moment before he answered. Then he smiled and said it was not, and asked her if she would come and dance.

The music was inviting. His company even more so.

Catherine said yes.

24

obert and Susanna returned to Madderly Castle on Monday, the twenty-second day of December. Less than an hour after their arrival, Robert forced his way into the study, closing the door behind him to closet himself with Lord Madderly.

Lord Madderly rose from his Glastonbury chair, so incensed that the pointed beard in the center of his chin began to quiver. "Leave at once, sir. You have no business here."

"I am the queen's agent," Robert announced.

After a moment's hesitation, Madderly sank back onto a well-padded seat. His eyes shot daggers at the intruder, but there were no other weapons in sight. "I remember you when you were a lad in the old duke of Northumberland's retinue. Troublemakers, all of you."

"But loyal to the Crown." During the next silent, tense

moments, Robert assessed his adversary. Madderly was overweight and at least ten years older than Robert. Once honey-
color hair was going gray, as was the bodkin beard.

Madderly glowered, but said only, "What do you want?"

Robert relaxed slightly. Although he carried no visible sign
of his injuries, his arm was still too stiff to allow for much
movement. Fighting was not a viable option.

"You collect letters as well as books and maps, my lord.
Why is that?"

"Why should I not?"

"Because someone is counterfeiting seals and forging signatures and using them for treasonous purposes."

"By Saint Anthony's Fire, you abuse me! I have no part in
any treason."

"You are the most likely suspect," Robert disagreed. "You
have access to the signatures and seals on those letters. Even
the royal seal."

Madderly began to sweat. "The aumbry in which I keep
my collection of letters is not locked. Anyone could borrow
what is within." He looked appalled by the prospect of be-
trayal within his household and terrified at the idea of being
formally accused himself, but he did not venture to name
any names.

"You've no knowledge of any forged documents?" Robert
asked. "Passports? Bills of exchange?"

"None."

"What of the counterfeit genealogy your wife produced
before your marriage?"

Madderly started at the mention of Eleanor. "What mean
you, Sir Robert? Speak plain or I will call my men and have
you evicted from this place, queen's man or no."

"We have just returned from Elnestow, my lord. No one there has ever heard of a Radcliffe named Eleanor."

"Nonsense. I have seen her genealogy myself. And I have letters from her father."

"You have, I suspect, naught but forgeries."

Briefly, Madderly was silent. Then he huffed and stood. "Come with me," he ordered, and led the way into the library proper.

From a locked, brass-bound chest, he withdrew a wooden box, ornately carved. "Here is a herald's account of Eleanor's family, together with several letters written by Sir Humphrey to his daughter at the time of her marriage to me."

Unconvinced, Robert began to leaf through the papers. All fake, he assumed, but he read their contents with interest. If what he and Susanna had worked out was right, this box contained naught but fictitious documents sealed with forgeries of the official seals.

"Eleanor would have done better to follow the example of a family of my acquaintance and manufacture proof of her descent from some previously unknown son of a long-ago nobleman." They'd also appropriated a fourteenth-century tomb in the local church and laid on a series of forged family brasses in the chancel to represent three centuries' worth of fictitious ancestors. "It is impossible for Eleanor to be Sir Humphrey Radcliffe's daughter, my lord. Sir Humphrey was a mere boy the year she was born. And he has been married but once, to his present wife."

Madderly started to object, but Robert cut him short.

"Your proof of her lineage is patently false. I say you knew that already. How could you not know she lied about her family?"

"I did not know. I do not know it now."

"Have you ever met her so-called father?"

Madderly hesitated, then shook his head. "No. She was estranged from her family."

"Convenient."

"What has this to do with treason, Sir Robert?"

"I believe your wife was murdered because she had some connection to the counterfeiters Lord Glenelg was involved with in his treason." Details of the plot were obscure, but the queen's agents knew enough to give Robert his orders. "After Glenelg was murdered, your wife likely guessed the killer's identity."

"She said naught to me." Abruptly, he turned his back and stalked off toward the study. Robert followed.

"Then why go to such extremes to make it seem the two murders were unconnected? You are the one who insisted two separate killers exist."

Back in Madderly's study with the door closed once more, the baron collapsed into his chair, all the fight gone out of him. "I admit it crossed my mind that my wife might have killed Lord Glenelg, but not until after she, too, was killed. She was most agitated the night Glenelg died and she had ample time to do the deed before supper."

"What motive did you think she had?"

But Madderly had said all he intended to. Robert's suspicion grew that Lord Glenelg, working with the same counterfeiters who'd prepared Eleanor's genealogy, had learned her secret. Had she killed him to keep her antecedents secret? He frowned and addressed the widower.

"If, as you believe, your wife killed Lord Glenelg, then who killed her? And why?"

"I know not."

"No thief?"

Lord Madderly winced at Robert's sarcasm. "I sought to avoid scandal when I encouraged local officials to accept my theory that two outsiders were responsible." A beseeching note came into his voice. He suddenly looked far older than his years. "You must see I had no choice. A man must protect his family's reputation."

Robert's frown deepened. He was not convinced yet that Lord Madderly was being honest with him, but he had another question to ask. "Tell me about Gilbert Russell. He is no more a native of Stratford-upon-Avon than I am."

On this score, Madderly was more forthcoming. He seemed relieved at the change of subject, but not surprised. "Russell was sent to me by an acquaintance. He asked me to take the fellow into my household."

"Has this acquaintance a name?"

Madderly hesitated, then mumbled, "Tom Randolph."

"The queen's ambassador to Scotland?"

"Aye. He swore me to secrecy, but since you are both the queen's agents . . ." His voice trailed off as he realized he'd seen no proof that Robert was who he claimed to be.

Robert set aside for the moment the troubling possibility that Gilbert Russell might be working for Randolph. "Let us suppose," he said smoothly, "that he is the killer. That he not only murdered Lord Glenelg and Lady Madderly but also hired someone to kill me two days past, injuring my wife in the attempt."

He lied without a qualm. Susanna's limp was worse and Robert meant to make use of that fact. He would see who seemed curious about it, and who alarmed. He did not believe anyone had intended her to be harmed.

"You think Russell responsible?" Madderly still sounded doubtful.

"Why not? For all we know, that is not even his real name. And if he brought a letter from Tom Randolph—" Madderly nodded. "Well, that may be yet another forgery."

Madderly heaved himself out of his chair and began to pace. "It was Gilbert Russell who suggested to me that an old enemy of Glenelg's might have killed him."

"Possible," Robert mused, "but not likely. Now, here is what you are going to do if you wish to prove your loyalty to the queen."

He spent the next half hour convincing Madderly that Susanna knew nothing about the suspected treason, that she'd been sent solely to provide her husband with a convenient excuse to visit Madderly Castle and stay through the holidays, and that she would remain when he left only to complete the herbal. In truth, if he'd not found all the answers he sought by the day after Twelfth Night, she would remain behind to continue the investigation.

He felt well pleased with himself when he reported all that had passed between them to Susanna a short time later, but she looked skeptical. She seemed even less impressed with his request that she continue to limp for at least another day or two so that he could observe how others reacted to her disability.

"If I was the intended target, remorse or guilt may appear when the killer realizes you were hurt by mistake."

"I do not believe this person can be so easily tricked into

betraying himself. Or herself. And I do much doubt someone who has killed twice will care that others are accidentally injured."

"Have you any better plan?"

"No. Only more questions. Who was Eleanor if not the Radcliffe she claimed? And who is Gilbert Russell?"

"The last," he assured her, "is one I mean to ask Tom Randolph as soon as I return to Edinburgh."

25

On Christmas Eve the festivities began in earnest when the Yule log was brought into the great hall, set upon the fire-dogs in the fireplace, and lit.

"To good luck for all and long feasting!" shouted the King of the Bean.

A roar of approval went up. An evening of feasting, singing, and dancing lay ahead, and even the presence of Susanna and Robert and the watchful eye they kept on Gilbert Russell could not mar Catherine's happiness.

At first she stayed close to the fire, for she enjoyed watching it while listening to the viols and rebecs. She was in the wrong place, however, when a sudden downdraft sent a gust of smoke into the room.

"Smoke will to the snicker," the King of the Bean announced when she began to cough.

"What means he by that?" she asked.

" 'Tis a compliment, lass." Otto Harleigh peered at her through bleary eyes, already the worse for several tankards of ale. " 'Tis an old belief in these parts. When maids cluster about the hearth on a windy day and smoke is blown down into the room, the smoke always seeks out the prettiest face. A snicker is a pretty girl."

"Then 'tis a true saying." Gilbert eased Otto out of the way and took his place beside Catherine, smiling at her fondly and capturing her hand to plant a kiss on her wrist.

Flattered and flustered, Catherine could think of nothing to say. That Gilbert thought her pretty kept her heart light through most of the evening, though they were soon separated by others at the party.

As she had the previous Sunday, she danced with any who asked. There were no distinctions between servants and gentlefolk at Yuletide. A few tried to take advantage, but Catherine knew where the mistletoe had been hung and steered deftly away from it.

Only Master Wheelwright, finely dressed in a good-quality black taffeta doublet with many close-set, intricately carved buttons, succeeded in maneuvering her beneath the kissing bough. His mouth was wet and his beard scratched her face and she did not like being kissed that way by a man so much older than herself. She persuaded him to fetch her a cup of sack, hoping to avoid being kissed by him a second time.

"Psst!" The sound came from behind her.

Startled, Catherine looked around and finally located Gilbert, partly concealed by a tapestry. "Are you hiding from someone, Master Russell?"

"I am lurking, hoping to spirit you away."

"You would have me leave the fun? Why, the mummers have yet to arrive."

"I can offer you better entertainment. Besides, the mummers will not come until tomorrow. First we shall feast and then, after the plum pudding, there will be a great knocking on the door and in will come the King of the Bean and all his retinue and the mummers, too."

"Will they play Saint George and the Dragon?" Catherine asked as she allowed him to pull her into the window embrasure behind the tapestry. They were cocooned there in a small, private world of their own.

"Indeed they will. I am told it lasts a full half hour and there are five characters in it: Father Christmas, Saint George, a Turkish knight, a doctor, and an old woman."

"What? No dragon?" She sat on the window seat, arranging her skirts in a way that would keep him at a respectable distance should he decide to join her.

"Disguises are part of the season."

His enigmatic smile made Catherine uneasy. Susanna had been at great pains to relay all her suspicions about Gilbert. "I know not what you mean."

With a shrug, he changed the subject, leaning idly against the window frame and looking down at her. In the dimness, he was a looming shadow, but she felt no trepidation, only a kind of gentle excitement. Susanna had to be wrong about this man.

"What has caused Lady Appleton to limp?" he asked. "A most strange limp, for it becomes much worse whenever she is aware of someone watching her."

Guilty color flooded into Catherine's face. She hoped it

was too dark for him to notice. "My fault," she whispered. "Because of me she was sorely hurt two years ago."

"How?"

"A fall."

"How your fault?"

For a moment Catherine hesitated. Then she told him. All of it, including the true identity of her father.

Gilbert was very quiet when she stopped speaking. She dared not look up and meet his eyes. What if he thought her actions in keeping her inheritance deceitful? Susanna insisted she was Randall Denholm's rightful heir, related by blood or not, but sometimes Catherine had doubts.

"It must have been a difficult time for you," Gilbert said at last. Then he sat down close beside her, gently moving the fabric of her widespread skirts out of his way.

She looked up then, into sympathetic blue eyes.

He began to talk of his own past, though in frustratingly vague terms. His mother, he said, had been estranged from her family because she'd married for love. Listening carefully, Catherine heard the emotion behind what he was saying. He'd loved his mother deeply, and resented her father and brother, who had cut her off without a penny.

Surely Robert and Susanna were mistaken about Gilbert, Catherine thought. Every feminine instinct she possessed told her she and Gilbert had something special between them. She was certain he would never harm her or anyone she cared about.

But he had lied about his origins in Warwickshire. Catherine was torn. She was tempted to take Gilbert to task for this lie, but at the same time she wanted him to tell her the truth without her asking. She thought he might be about to when he leaned close.

Instead, he settled his lips over hers in a kiss that was nothing like the sloppy effort Master Wheelwright had made. This kiss felt very good indeed, and it ended much too soon.

"Lady Appleton is looking for you," Gilbert whispered. From his vantage point he could just see through the opening at the side of the tapestry. "Do you wish to be found?"

"I do not know," Catherine answered honestly.

With obvious reluctance, Gilbert released her and stood. "Best I leave first. Count to one hundred before you come after me, and peep out first to be sure you are not observed."

He was gone before she could respond.

The air of delicious secrecy went with him. The alcove was no longer imbued with romance. Their hiding place suddenly seemed tawdry. Had she done wrong to be alone with him? She even wondered if she should run straight to Susanna and confess her indiscretion.

Confused, she remained where she was for a long time, trying to make sense of her emotion. She must be in love, she finally decided. Nothing else could explain this strange division of loyalties, or this terrible uncertainty about what was in her own mind.

26

ood maarning, ma'am. How bist, zur? 'Tis maartle cold this day." Nan bustled into the room to light the fire. " 'Tis th' virst of January, when th' ship be brought down vrom th' uplands vor better leaze."

"Ship? What ship?" Robert mumbled sleepily. "Gloucester is an inland county."

"She means sheep, my dear."

"Then why did she not say so?"

"What is leaze, Nan?"

"Pasture, ma'am."

"Ah, yes." She turned to Robert, who was now rubbing the sleep from his eyes. "Here they do also call a field ground and the wood is a conger, since it is the abode of the cony. A fence or a stone wall is a mound."

"Stwun," Nan corrected.

"Yes. Stwun, not stone."

Robert was not impressed. "Tell me the word for ale and have done, woman."

Susanna yawned and stretched as Nan bustled off to fetch ale. "New Year's Day. You will be leaving in less than a week and we have accomplished so little."

"I must go. To allay suspicion. You will be safe enough if you are subtle about your questions."

"And in Scotland you can question Tom Randolph about Gilbert and search again for Peadar."

He did not respond to that. In fact, he would tell her nothing more, but she knew it disturbed him that there was a possibility the queen might be playing two of her diplomats against each other, testing them to see which could solve a case of treason first.

Feeling unaccountably glum, Susanna rose and began to dress. The day would be a busy one and should be full of cheer. After all, New Year's Day was set aside for a general exchange of gifts.

In the evening there would be wassailing and healths. Tenants and friends would flock to the castle and assemble around a huge bowl of spiced ale called "lamb's wool" and as it went from hand to hand, each drinker would shout "wassail!" as the ancient Saxons had. Then the poor folk would be let in, each carrying a big wooden bowl tied with ribbons, and the steward would fill them up with ale, too.

The festivities would continue until Twelfth Night, the eve of Robert's departure for Scotland, when there would be bonfires in the grainfields. The people would drink more healths and that night they would also toast their oxen. She wondered if the same tradition was followed here as she'd seen in other places. The women of the manor baked an enormous cake, which was taken to the barn. After draughts of strong ale had been drunk to each of the beasts within, the cake was set in the horns of the biggest ox. The owner then tickled his nose with a straw until he tossed his head and flung the cake to the ground. Men and boys alike scrambled to pick up the pieces, then rushed back to the manor house for one last night of song and dance and eating and drinking.

Suddenly Susanna felt very homesick. She missed Leigh Abbey, especially at this time of year. It would fall to Mark and Jennet to keep the old traditions in the home Susanna had inherited from her father.

Then she smiled. Yuletide was something they all shared, no matter how it was celebrated, and so was a sense of home and hearth. What was it Nan had told her when they'd chanced upon the house she'd grown up in on their way out of Campden after Eleanor's funeral?

"There I were born, an' my vather, an' his, an' his avoor 'un. Us lived in this pleace an' brute health were our portion."

There were worse dowries.

27

That is very good, Mistress Catherine." John Wheelwright sounded as if he genuinely admired the apple she was carving from a piece of soft wood.

The accomplishment had not come without cost. Yet another thin line of blood on one finger betrayed the slip of her sharp little knife. Catherine lifted the injured digit to her mouth and sucked on the cut.

Wheelwright's dark eyes grew warm as he watched her. She dropped her gaze, reluctant to encourage him further. Wheelwright was not unattractive, but he was much too old to suit her. At least fifty. And there were streaks of gray in his short, pointed chin beard. Besides, her heart belonged to Gilbert Russell.

"What of my rabbit?" Edward demanded, holding up the figure he had been working on.

"Why, Edward," Catherine exclaimed with genuine pleasure. "How talented you are. You could be a woodcarver if you ever needed to earn your way in the world."

"I shall be a baron," Edward informed her. "I will have no need to work."

Philip frowned. "Will I have to?"

"Never fear," said Catherine. "I am sure your father will provide well for you, too."

"Could I be paid for carving?" Philip held up the tiny lump of wood which remained. With charity, he might be said to have made the shape of a dog.

"You will need to practice a great deal first," Catherine said honestly. "And mayhap you would have to learn to carve in stone instead. Big pieces that people put in their gardens."

"Or headstones," Master Wheelwright suggested.

Catherine sent a quelling look in his direction, then realized that since he had been the one to teach them all to carve in the first place he was doubtless a master of the art himself. She had seen none of his completed efforts, but it seemed likely he was a perfectionist. He must find all their poor attempts most pitiful.

Catherine and the boys worked in silence for a time, putting finishing touches on the articles they intended for gifts on this New Year's Day. In addition to the apple, which was for Susanna, Catherine had made what she hoped looked like a cat. She planned to give that to Gilbert Russell. A flower of indeterminate species was for Magdalen. She'd hemmed and embroidered handkerchiefs for the remainder of her gifts.

Another nick in her finger made her decide the apple looked as fine as it ever would. She brushed wood shavings off her skirt and paused to tickle Bede between the ears. He seemed more at ease with her now. Sometimes he even tolerated being cuddled.

In the distance, a church bell rang the hour. John Wheelwright rose from his chair. "I've a personal matter to see to," he said and left the schoolroom.

Edward started to chuckle. "I wager he has a gift for you, Catherine. He wants you to kiss him again."

"Nonsense." But Catherine blushed.

"You could marry him," Philip said. "Then you could stay here forever and help tutor us."

"We have little in common aside from a love of learning," Catherine pointed out.

"You come from the same part of England," Edward said.

Puzzled, Catherine tucked the finished wooden apple into a pocket and gave the boy a questioning look. "That is not sufficient reason to marry, either. And I do not know why you should think so. I cannot remember ever mentioning the county of my origin to you boys, or to your schoolmaster, either."

" 'Tis the way you both say certain words," Edward informed her. " 'Tis not the Gloucestershire way, nor from London, either."

"What words?" Catherine had thought her speech quite refined by these last two years in Kent. And she'd heard little of the north in Master Wheelwright's speech. Still, he could have come from Lancashire originally.

"Stone," Edward said promptly.

To illustrate he said the word three ways, first with the true kind of pronunciation of the royal court, then the

Gloucestershire way, and last in imitation of Catherine herself. And of John Wheelwright when he'd muttered the word *headstone.*

"Mayhap Master Wheelwright was just making fun of my way of speaking," Catherine suggested. She'd noticed no other slips. Of course, she was usually more careful herself, having an aversion to becoming an object of ridicule.

"There are other words you say oddly," Edward informed her.

"Then you have a good ear for accents. Better than mine own."

"Drums. You say that word wrong. And poor. And sometimes book."

A stray memory brought a frown to Catherine's face. Someone else in this household *had* said the word *book* in the northern way. But who? She did not think it had been John Wheelwright, though it might have been.

She would have to ask him someday whence he hailed, and hope he did not take the question as evidence of an increasing personal interest in him. She did not want to have to fend off another kiss.

28

Magdalen Harleigh came into the library as she always did and went straight to the hiding place she'd devised after Lord Glenelg found her manuscript. She knew at once that something was wrong. Her papers had been disturbed.

"Are you looking for this?" Susanna Appleton asked.

Turning slowly, Magdalen regarded the gentlewoman with suspicion. In Lady Appleton's hand was Magdalen's treasure, the work of her heart, the secret she had been trying to keep from everyone since she'd learned the hard way that revealing it only led to ridicule.

"They are very fine," Lady Appleton said.

"I do not believe you."

"Why should you not?" Genuine astonishment underscored the question.

"Please, return those pages to me and speak no more of them. They represent an impossible dream."

"To see them in print? To let others read what you have created? 'Tis not so impossible, Magdalen."

"Please, I—"

"Who has told you these poems were unworthy? Ah, never mind. No need to answer. 'Twas your husband who mocked them, was it not? He has made you feel that these are mere scribblings, a bastard child to be hidden away from the world."

Magdalen felt herself flush. She could not deny the accuracy of Lady Appleton's guess. At the same time, a faint glimmer of hope began to grow. Could she possibly mean what she'd said? Could these posies be better than Otto had thought? And did Lady Appleton speak from firsthand knowledge of a husband's power to undermine self-confidence? Sir Robert had left right after Twelfth Night and his wife had seemed much happier since.

"Who else knows you have been writing poetry?" she asked.

"Only my husband. And Lord Glenelg may have seen. I caught him going through my papers once, but I do not think he'd had time to read what was written upon them. He tried to make me think I'd done something disloyal to Lord Madderly, even though he had no way to know the words were mine. For all he knew, they might have been copied out of another's book of verses." She frowned, thoughtful. Mayhap that was what he had believed. Had he been accusing her of stealing another's work?

She looked up to find a matching frown on Lady Appleton's face.

"I did not kill him for that," Magdalen added quickly. "Only found a new hiding place for my papers."

A little silence fell. Then Lady Appleton said, "You've guessed I have not abandoned my quest for the killer."

"Aye." Magdalen sighed deeply. " 'Tis unwise, I do think, to ask questions so openly."

"I had thought I was being subtle."

Magdalen just looked at her.

"Never mind that. For the moment, let us discuss what is to be done about these." She tapped the sheets of foolscap in her hand. "May I send them to the printer who published my book? I think he will be interested."

"But will he not balk at reading the work of a woman?"

"I cannot see why he should. He has already read a woman's work. Mine. And my cautionary herbal is making money for him. Why should he object to making more through your efforts?"

"But no other woman has had original poetry published. Has she?"

"Not that we know of, yet I've heard it theorized by certain well-educated ladies of my acquaintance that Anonymous may well have been a woman. Even if she was not, there is no reason why you should not be published. Stop scratching your arm. You will get an infection."

"Oh!"

"I will make you a salve of Saracen's root, Saint John's-wort, Herb of the Sun, serpent's tongue, and oil of lavender, the same one I once gave to the late king of France to soothe his itching. You must apply it twice a day and wrap your fingers if you cannot stay them from digging."

Magdalen looked down at her hands, at the bright flecks of

blood beneath the fingernails, and sighed again. "When I am nervous, I do not realize what I am doing till 'tis done."

"A calming brew to drink will not be amiss, either. Perhaps a mixture of chamomile, skullcap, Saint John's-wort, and Holy Herb."

Before Magdalen knew what had happened, Lady Appleton had rearranged her life. By the time the two women parted company a few hours later, the poems were already on their way to London by special messenger and Magdalen felt as if she could walk on clouds.

She abruptly fell to earth when she returned to her bedchamber to store Lady Appleton's remedies in her medicine chest and found Beatrice waiting. "What are you doing here?" Magdalen demanded.

"Examining the size of your rooms."

"Why?"

"There must be some changes, now that Eleanor is gone." With her sister-by-marriage dead, Beatrice was in charge of all domestic matters at Madderly Castle save the herbal.

What did she have in mind? Magdalen wondered. Smaller rooms? A bed in an alcove off the kitchens? Magdalen had long since sensed that Beatrice disliked and resented her, but she had not thought to find the enmity extended to this degree. It was not as if Magdalen had been the one to take the prize of completing the herbal from Beatrice. The noblewoman did not have that reason to take petty revenge on a mere waiting gentlewoman. Magdalen could only conclude that Beatrice was doing this out of plain mean-spiritedness.

Fuming silently, Magdalen managed not to blurt out any harsh accusations. She went about her business, locking away the salve and the herbs for the calming brew. She was about to depart when the door opened again to admit Otto. Magdalen gaped at him, startled to see him. Her husband never came to their rooms during the day. Or did he? Since Magdalen herself rarely visited them at this hour, it was possible he regularly slipped away from the stables and slept off his nightly excesses during the day.

"What are you doing here, wife?" he demanded.

Instead of cowering, she took Lady Appleton for a model and answered back. "You'd do better to ask why she has come." Magdalen gestured toward Beatrice. The thought that the two of them had arranged to meet flickered through her mind but she quickly dismissed it. What would Beatrice want with Otto? She thought much too highly of herself to deign to seduce a servant.

"I am chatelaine of this castle." Beatrice touched the keys hanging from her girdle to emphasize the point and by her haughty manner confirmed Magdalen's opinion that an affair between Otto and Beatrice was most unlikely.

Another thought banished such speculation entirely. Beatrice had been chatelaine in all but name for years. Could resentment over that alone have been reason enough to do away with Eleanor? Had Beatrice killed her?

That appalling thought made Magdalen cautious. She supposed anyone could kill, given enough provocation. While she'd been stowing the medical supplies she'd also been envisioning how pleasant it would be to run Beatrice through with a letter opener. What if Beatrice had struck out, in anger or with deliberate malice, to remove an obstacle from her path?

If she had done so once, she might do so again. Magdalen abruptly decided she had too much to live for to let herself become the next victim.

"I wish you joy of these chambers," she told Beatrice as she swept from the room. She almost enjoyed the look of consternation on Otto's face. Let *him* talk Beatrice out of her plan to evict them if he objected to it.

In the cool, stone-lined corridor, she stopped to lean against the closed door and catch her breath. She could hear nothing of what was being said inside. The door's wooden panels were too thick to let anything but a murmur of sound escape. Otto might be in amicable conversation with Beatrice or at daggers drawn. To her own surprise, Magdalen realized she did not care what happened between them.

Lady Appleton had shown her there was more to life than trying to please an impossible husband.

29

You must warn me if you hear footsteps," Susanna told Catherine. "I do not care to be discovered tearing the workroom apart. 'Twould look suspicious."

Most especially, she did not want to be caught by Beatrice, not after what Magdalen had told her of the other woman's apparent plan to take petty revenge for Magdalen's devotion to Eleanor by removing the Harleighs from gracious rooms and relegating them to small, uncomfortable lodgings over the stables. That this had not yet happened both women attributed to Otto Harleigh's value to Lord Madderly. The master of horse was an important officer in the household. He had no doubt used his influence to stay Beatrice's hand.

" 'Tis suspicious enough that we are here this late at night," Catherine said in a carrying whisper.

"We can always claim we could not sleep and decided to spend more time working on the herbal."

Methodically, she rapped on each section of paneling, listening for a hollow sound. Magdalen's use of more than one hiding place for her poems had made Susanna realize that Eleanor might have done the same. That there was a missing notebook seemed certain. She'd at first assumed it had been found and destroyed, but now she thought perhaps it had not been. If it was hidden in this room, she meant to find it tonight.

Her search was rewarded only moments after she began. It took somewhat longer to find the catch to release the section of linenfold paneling so that it opened out into the room. Within, wrapped in oilskin, was another of the leather-bound notebooks Eleanor had used to write down her thoughts on the preparation of her herbal.

Almost reverently, Susanna removed it from its hiding place. She was peripherally aware that Catherine had entered the workroom and was watching with anticipation equal to her own. Susanna's fingers trembled slightly as she unwrapped their prize, opened the book, and began to read.

Catherine moved closer to look over her shoulder. "Why this contains nothing more than notes on the weather!"

"So it does seem, but I'll wager Leigh Abbey that this notebook holds a secret message of some sort."

"A code?" Catherine's eyes sparkled with anticipation. "Can you translate it?"

"I am sure I will be able to, given enough time. This much I can tell you already—the first entry was written on the day after Lord Glenelg died. That is significant in itself." So was the fact that Eleanor had hidden the notebook.

But try as she would, after they removed to their own chambers, Susanna found no key to the code that night. The next day brought more frustration until she finally set aside the task, hoping inspiration would strike while she was away from it.

30

Exactly two weeks after Robert left Madderly Castle for Scotland, Susanna received a letter from him. Catherine noted the grim look on her face as she began to decode it and sent a silent prayer heavenward that it would prove easier than Lady Madderly's notebook. That still remained an enigma days after they'd found it.

Three hours later, Susanna put her quill aside to stare at the parchment. Idly, she toyed with the carved apple Catherine had given her. Her brow furrowed.

"Gilbert Russell," she muttered.

Catherine abandoned her embroidery. "What about Gilbert?"

"Bodykins." Plainly Susanna had forgotten Catherine's presence. " 'Tis naught," she said hastily. Too hastily.

" 'Tis something."

Relenting, Susanna crossed to the window seat and settled in at Catherine's side. "Gilbert has been misrepresenting himself," she said gently. "You already knew he was no simple son of Warwickshire merchants."

"Who is he then?" She held her breath.

"Robert has discovered that Gilbert is Lord Glenelg's heir, the missing nephew. In truth Gilbert Russell has been Gilleabart, ninth baron Glenelg, ever since the eighth baron's murder."

Catherine's first reaction was dismay. What if her inheritance was not sufficient to tempt a nobleman? Then she caught sight of Susanna's face. She had no difficulty reading her mentor's thoughts. Gaining a title and estate would be motive aplenty for killing a man.

"No," she said firmly. "He would not."

"The ring with his crest was found clutched in Eleanor's hand. The knife that killed Glenelg and then disappeared bore the same crest."

"And that in itself should make you realize he must be innocent. If he took such trouble to remove the bye-knife from the body, why wear a ring with the same crest? And how could he not know Eleanor had ripped it from his finger? He'd have taken it back ere he left the tower workroom. Mayhap," she added, "the ring is a counterfeit. Is that possible?"

"It is possible," Susanna conceded, "but unlikely. Robert says the conspirators we are looking for copy signets in wood, for only the impression on a seal is needed in their forgeries."

"Then the ring you found must have been stolen from Lord Glenelg's effects? Oh!"

"What?"

"Ask Gilbert to try it on. If it does not fit, then it was old Lord Glenelg's and not Gilbert's at all."

"I do not want anyone to know I have the ring," Susanna reminded her.

"Why wait when revealing it can prove or disprove innocence?"

"And if it fits his finger? What then, Catherine? 'Tis not enough proof to order his arrest, only enough to alert him to our suspicions and place ourselves in danger."

'Twould also be most unfair to Gilbert, Catherine thought, for revealing what they knew would surely damn him in the eyes of the rest of the household. Here was a quandary indeed.

"Do you want him to be guilty?" She knew she sounded sulky. "That way you would be certain I could not have him."

"Be sensible, Catherine. A Scots baron will look to the Scots nobility for a wife. You are . . . the daughter of a Lancashire gentleman."

"He knows who I am." Catherine struck a defiant pose. "I told him on Christmas Eve."

"What!"

"Aye. Well, you know he thought I was Sir Robert's bastard child." Miserable again, she bowed her head and lowered her voice. "I did not care for that, so I told him the truth. All of it."

"And his reaction?"

"He was surprised, but he did not think less of me for my parents' folly." And that gave Catherine hope that he, like Sir Humphrey Radcliffe with his Isabelle, might be inclined to overlook the differences in their station. If he loved her enough, he might yet ask her to be his wife.

Her own distress plain, Susanna took Catherine's hands in hers. "I wish you had not been so trusting."

217

"You do not like Gilbert," Catherine complained. "You have never liked him."

"On the contrary. I see very well what it is in him that appeals to you. The same qualities appeal to any woman with warm blood in her veins. That is the problem. I am old enough to wonder how much of his true nature he keeps hidden beneath that charming facade. I do not know what he is capable of. For your sake, Catherine, I would like to believe he is an honorable man, a man with a deep sense of family, devoted to his kin."

"But you don't." Sarcasm slipped out. "And if you did, why, then you would only argue that Eleanor killed Lord Glenelg because he knew about her past and Gilbert murdered her to avenge his uncle!"

To Catherine's horror, Susanna looked as if she was considering that possibility.

"Gilbert Russell is not the sort of man who could do dark deeds. He is far too honorable. Look at the way he constantly evades my advances!"

Too late, she realized how much she'd revealed. Clapping both hands over her mouth, she stared at Susanna through wide eyes.

"Advances?" Susanna's voice was too quiet. "Catherine, have you done more than flirt with him?"

Hot color seeped into her face. "Only one kiss."

With a sigh to equal any of Mistress Harleigh's, Susanna briefly closed her eyes. When she opened them again, her gaze was implacable. "You are henceforth to avoid being alone with Gilbert Russell," she decreed. "He is a suspect in two violent murders. If you cannot keep away from him of your own volition, I will be obliged to send you back to Kent."

Catherine sprang to her feet. "You cannot send me anywhere I do not want to go. You yourself taught me that I am mistress of mine own fate. And that I may marry any man I will."

"I had also hoped I'd taught you common sense," Susanna muttered.

Catherine's pleasure in having made her point abruptly vanished.

31

The rift between Catherine and Susanna grew wider with each passing day and Susanna did not know how to bridge it. She could not come out and accuse Gilbert Russell publicly of murder. She had no proof. As yet, she had not even revealed to any but Catherine that he was the new Lord Glenelg.

For her part, Catherine defiantly seized every opportunity to seek out Gilbert's company. Fortunately, he seemed as anxious to avoid being alone with her as Susanna could desire. It was not that he was not attracted to her. Susanna feared he was. But he had a modicum of that common sense Catherine lacked.

Perhaps he sensed the power of Lady Appleton's wrath should he harm her chick in any way.

Carrying two heavy tomes, Susanna left the library for the workroom. Catherine, recruited for that specific task, followed her carrying two more. A sulky expression took away the natural beauty of her features.

Be civil, Susanna warned herself. Naught could be gained by badgering the girl. Indeed, a neutral topic of conversation seemed wise.

"This matter of illustrations for the herbal troubles me," she said as they crossed to the workroom tower. "Many of these books of healing use the same woodcuts. Master Lonicer's *Kreuterbuck* simply copies, crudely colored, the pictures from Leonhard Fuchsias's *Icones Plantarum.*"

"So does Master Turner's *New Herbal,*" Catherine replied. Since that book was in English, she had been assigned to check references in it.

"What disturbs me even more is the fact that these drawings are so stylized that the plants are reduced to symmetrical patterns of leaves, branches, and flowers. No one seeing the real herb growing wild would recognize it."

"I have been reading Master Turner with interest," Catherine said. "He talks much of astrological lore. And of a man called Paracelsus, who seems to use minerals and what he calls chemical medicines in his cures. I had thought plants were the only medicines, and that Dioscorides was the infallible authority on them."

"No one is infallible." More proof of that was before her. The workroom door, which she had left closed, was standing open. Someone was inside, noisily rifling through the contents of one of the chests.

For a moment Susanna's nerve almost failed her. This was an eerie reversal of the way she'd found Eleanor's body. Then she drew a breath and stepped into the room.

Even before she could accuse him, Edward spoke. "We were not doing anything wrong."

Philip offered a variation on that theme. " 'Tisn't my fault. He made me come with him."

"What are you boys doing here?" Susanna asked.

"This is my father's castle," Edward informed her in a haughty voice. "I may go where I please."

Hands on her hips, Susanna stared the older boy down. When he looked away, she glanced quickly at Catherine and was in time to catch a fleeting smile. Amused herself, Susanna still insisted on an answer. "Well? What were you looking for? I can assure you that there are no obscene pictures here."

Only slightly abashed, Edward stood his ground. "We are looking for your flying spell. Old Mother Coddington told Aunt Beatrice you likely had one, seeing as you are a witch."

"Bodykins!" Suddenly weak-kneed, Susanna sank down onto the stool in front of her worktable. The charge of practicing witchcraft could not be taken lightly, even though it was not a crime in England. In extreme cases, charges of heresy could still be brought in ecclesiastical court, and heresy was punishable by burning to death.

"What nonsense!" Catherine went so far as to seize Edward by the shoulders and give him a shake. "Lady Appleton is no more a witch than Mother Coddington is. They are experts on plants. No more. And you should know better than to eavesdrop on two evil-minded gossips."

"I like Mother Coddington, even if she is a witch," Philip protested. "She showed cook how to make candied horehound cubes for us."

"Witch or not, she does not know Lady Appleton, and she was wrong to malign her."

"Enough, Catherine," Susanna interrupted. "I would know exactly what the boys overheard."

"Mother Coddington met Aunt Beatrice in the stable," Philip said.

"A secret meeting." Edward lowered his voice. "They did not know we were there. Mother Coddington gave Aunt Beatrice a cloth-wrapped packet and Aunt Beatrice gave her some coins. Then Aunt Beatrice said, 'Would I could as easily rid myself of all who are unwelcome.'"

Catherine's sharply indrawn breath told Susanna that she understood the implication the boys had missed.

"Go on," Susanna urged.

"Mother Coddington mumbled something about our stepmother. She must have talked to Mother Coddington about you, Lady Appleton."

"That is not so surprising, since we all share an interest in herbs."

In an effort to remember more, Edward scrunched up his forehead and squeezed his eyes shut. "She said it was not wise to know too much about herbs that kill. Then Aunt Beatrice said perhaps you needed a dose of your own medicine, and Mother Coddington said Aunt Beatrice would be unwise to challenge you because 'twas likely you were a witch as well as a cunning woman."

"Cunning woman I am," Susanna acknowledged, "for that title implies little more than a healer. But witch I am not nor ever have been. I do not cast spells or do harm."

"But what about the flying spell?" Philip, who had been listening avidly, eyes big, tugged on her sleeve to secure her attention.

"If I must guess what it was she referred to, then it is not a spell at all, but rather an ointment made from three deadly plants. Those who rub it on their bodies begin to hallucinate, to dream they are doing impossible things. They do not really fly, my dears. They only think that they are flying. And some who use too much of this ointment never wake up again at all. Any one of its ingredients alone contains enough poison to kill."

"There have been quite enough deaths in this house," Catherine told the boys. "Promise me you'll not try any dangerous experiments."

Solemnly, they gave their word, but after they left, Catherine turned to Susanna with worry in her eyes. "They are curious about herbs, knowing how much time Eleanor spent on her book. And they are young wildheads in the making."

"Perhaps," Susanna suggested, "since you seem to have a rapport with them, you should keep a close eye on their movements for the next few days."

Catherine gave her a sharp look, knowing full well that spending time in the schoolroom would limit the hours she could pass in pursuit of Gilbert Russell, but after a moment she nodded. "On this," she said, "we agree."

32

Catherine went to the schoolroom the following day for the express purpose of warning John Wheelwright that his charges had lately taken an interest in dangerous herbs. She supposed it had started with that business with the vitriol and gall, and now they both seemed uncommon interested in magic spells and witch's potions.

She was surprised to find no one there but Bede, and he was in the cage Master Wheelwright used when it was necessary to confine him. Intending to go to the window, which overlooked the archery butts, to see if the boys were practicing with bows and arrows, she was halfway across the room before she sensed something wrong about her surroundings. Coming to an abrupt halt she tried to pinpoint what had captured her attention. Furniture out of place? A window left open?

Then she saw it, a length of filmy fabric lying on the floor, disappearing behind a heavy, high-backed bench. For a moment she simply stared at it, unable to comprehend why it should be there.

She knew to whom it belonged. Beatrice often wore such decorations on her sleeves. Filled with sudden apprehension, Catherine tiptoed closer, until she could see what lay on the other side of the bench.

The far end of the fabric had been wrapped tight around Beatrice Madderly's neck. Catherine needed only one quick look to tell the noblewoman was dead. Her eyes and tongue bulged out. Her complexion was an ugly puce.

As slowly and quietly as she'd come, Catherine crept away, moving backward until she bumped up against the door. A squeak of alarm escaped her as it opened, pushing her forward again. She whirled to face the intruder. A scream caught in her throat as she recognized him.

Gilbert Russell held a small piece of foolscap in one hand and wore a puzzled expression on his face. He'd not expected to find Catherine here, of that she was certain.

"Where is Beatrice?" he asked, looking around.

"Thank God," Catherine whispered. If he was searching for Beatrice, then he did not know she was dead. He could not have been the one who killed her.

"Catherine?" His hands gripped her shoulders and he gave her a little shake. "What ails you, lass?"

"She's dead," Catherine whispered. "Beatrice is dead."

The next few minutes were a blur as Gilbert went to inspect the body, then came back to Catherine to lead her from the room. Somehow he got her back to her own chambers and sent Nan for Susanna. Once Lady Appleton arrived, the tension in the air increased tenfold.

"Another murder!" Susanna sounded appalled. "And you on the scene, Master Russell." She lowered her voice. "Or should I call you Lord Glenelg?"

"Is that why you are so suspicious of me, Lady Appleton?" he asked in a voice that betrayed no emotion beyond curiosity.

Susanna signaled Nan to leave them and the girl fled. By then, Catherine had gained possession of her wits. She wondered whether Nan would linger to listen at the door. Jennet would have.

"You were at a murder scene," Susanna said to Gilbert. "Right after the body was found. Again."

"*This* was sent to draw me to the place of Beatrice's death." He handed over the paper Catherine had noticed earlier. When Susanna had skimmed the contents, she passed it on to her younger friend.

It was a brief note, requesting Gilbert's immediate presence in the schoolroom. It was signed with Beatrice's name.

"A forgery, I presume," Gilbert said.

"He did not know she was dead. I'll swear it," Catherine put in. "Someone wanted him to be found with Beatrice's body and tricked him into going there. They did not count on my being there. I found her first."

A doubtful look on her face, Susanna considered this theory. "Or else he is a very clever man," she mused.

"You'd do better to suspect me," Catherine told her. "I had no cause to love Beatrice Madderly."

Gilbert gave her a considering look that made her breath catch. Surely he did not believe—

"Not strong enough," he decided.

She knew she should be grateful, but in truth she felt

a sudden urge to strangle him. Too weak? An insult. And that he should doubt her, even for a moment, upset her greatly until she recalled that, for a moment, she had also doubted him.

Hands on her hips, Susanna looked hard first at Gilbert, then at Catherine. "Who has been left with the body? Has the coroner been sent for? Has Lord—"

"Bodykins!" Catherine cried, appropriating the mild curse her mentor favored. "Someone must find Edward and Philip before they stumble on their aunt's body. No one is guarding it but Bede."

"By your leave, Lady Appleton?"

"Go, Gilbert. Do what must be done. But return when you can. You and I have matters to discuss."

"You cannot suspect Gilbert," Catherine said again when the two women were alone. "He had no reason to kill Beatrice. He was lured there."

"Why?" Susanna put firm hands on Catherine's shoulders and forced her to sit on the edge of the bed. She reached for the supply of herbs she'd had sent from Leigh Abbey with their clothing.

"No noxious brews!" Catherine refused to be treated like a child. "If you must physic me, then let it be with unwatered wine or good stale ale." The clearer the ale, the older it was, and the oldest was the most expensive. Catherine thought she deserved the top quality she'd requested.

Susanna poured a cup of sweet wine for Catherine and one for herself and watered neither. When she had settled herself comfortably at the head of the bed, pillows behind her and legs curled beneath her, she took a long swallow, lifted a questioning brow, and asked Catherine to give her a detailed account of all she had seen and done in the school-room.

"Who do you think killed Beatrice?" she asked when Catherine had dredged up every bit of information she could recall.

"Anyone but Gilbert."

Ticking them off on her fingers, Susanna listed the remaining possibilities. "Lord Madderly. Magdalen. Otto. Master Wheelwright."

"Do not forget Nan's demon." It seemed as likely as any of the others.

"What was Beatrice doing in the schoolroom?" Susanna asked. "I thought you told me once that she avoided the place."

"Aye. So she did. 'Tis curious she'd go there. And where were Master Wheelwright and the boys?"

"They were at the butts earlier," Susanna said, confirming Catherine's guess. With one gulp, she drained her cup. "I would see if they are there still. And ask a question or two. Are you coming?"

But before either woman could leave the chamber, they were delayed by the arrival of Magdalen Harleigh. "Is it true?" she asked. "Is Beatrice murdered?"

"Who told you that?" Susanna demanded.

"Your own tiring maid is saying it. Half the castle knows by now. Is it true?"

"Yes. And I cannot delay to tell you more. Only to ask you this. Did you see Beatrice this morning?"

Her face several shades paler than it had been a moment earlier, Magdalen swallowed hard and nodded. "Aye. She made a point of telling me she was on her way to the school-

231

room to meet someone. I had the most curious sense she was hinting she meant Otto, but that seemed unlikely since he was preparing to leave on a short trip to one of Lord Madderly's smaller properties. And what would Otto be doing in the schoolroom?"

Catherine opened her mouth, then closed it again. If Mistress Harleigh could not imagine what her husband might want with Beatrice Madderly, she'd not welcome hearing it from the lips of a young, unmarried woman. Beatrice and Otto! Otto giving Beatrice that love bite? Catherine had difficulty imagining it herself, but she liked this picture better than the one in which Gilbert and Beatrice were lovers.

"Have you seen Master Wheelwright today?" Susanna asked Magdalen.

"I saw the boys at archery practice perhaps an hour ago. I did not notice Master Wheelwright, but he must have been somewhere about. He never leaves them alone for long. They get into too much trouble."

John Wheelwright? As Susanna gave Magdalen a brief account of the discovery of Beatrice's body, Catherine considered. He had not liked Lord Glenelg, but she could think of no reason he'd want to harm either Lady Madderly or Beatrice. Susanna had told her he'd been with the boys when Lady Madderly died.

Catherine frowned. Susanna had also said that the boys were blindfolded, playing some game. Could Master Wheelwright have left them, raced up one flight of stairs, and killed Lady Madderly without their being aware of his absence? She supposed that was possible, but it didn't seem likely. Neither did the idea that Wheelwright would kill Beatrice in the schoolroom. Surely that would be the last place he'd choose if he were the murderer.

As much as Catherine wanted to find an alternate suspect to Gilbert, she could not think of a single reason why John Wheelwright would risk his position by killing three people. Besides, no one who could love Bede could possibly be a violent man. Otto seemed much more likely. Or Lord Madderly, who had always led Catherine's list of suspects.

"Come, Catherine," Susanna said, interrupting her thoughts. "I wish to speak with Master Wheelwright."

A few minutes later they were out-of-doors, watching Philip Madderly's miserable efforts to hit a target. His brother's taunts did not help Philip's aim. Both boys were so focused on improving their skill with the longbow that neither noticed they had an audience, not even when Susanna drew their tutor aside.

"You have been here some time, Master Wheelwright."

"Aye, Lady Appleton. 'Tis too fine a day to waste indoors."

"You have not returned to the schoolroom while the boys practiced?"

"And leave them armed and unsupervised?" But his smile faded under Susanna's penetrating stare.

Catherine felt almost sorry for him, faced with the full power of that formidable will. It did not surprise her that Wheelwright was the first to break eye contact. Looking a bit like a misbehaving schoolboy himself, he finally muttered an answer.

" 'Twas necessary for me to leave them briefly." He glanced at Catherine and quickly away. " 'Twas a . . . that is . . . er, 'twas a personal matter."

Catherine shared his embarrassment, but Susanna pushed harder. "Most men simply relieve themselves in the nearest corner."

"A bit of meat did not agree with me. 'Twas necessary to visit the jakes."

Susanna had to be satisfied with that, for she could delay no longer telling him of Catherine's grisly discovery. A commotion at the gatehouse told them the constable had arrived.

"Another murder!" Wheelwright seemed to Catherine to be genuinely appalled. His immediate concern for his young charges warmed her.

Susanna, however, watched him give them the news about their aunt with a jaundiced eye. To her, everyone remained suspect, even Gilbert.

They went next to confront Lord Madderly, catching up with him on his way to view his sister's body with the constable. Before Susanna could open her mouth, he waved her away. "Your husband may have authority to snoop," he said in a voice harsh with emotion, "but you do not. Get you back to your herbals or pack your bags and return home. I care not which."

Susanna and Catherine returned to their bedchamber, but not to pack. Susanna sent Nan for ale and bread and cheese. A few minutes after she left, Gilbert joined them.

"Ah, Lord Glenelg," Susanna greeted him.

"How long have you known?"

Catherine thought Gilbert seemed ill at ease with the title. She wanted to go to him, to offer support and comfort, but she remained where she was on the window seat, fearing that if she spoke in his defense again it would only make Susanna more determined to suspect him.

"Catherine and I have known you were the new Lord Glenelg since my husband sent word from Scotland, but we have told no one. Does anyone else here know who you really are?"

"No one anywhere knows but Peadar, mine uncle's manservant."

"And whoever told my husband. Who might that have been, Gilbert?"

Gilbert said nothing.

"Why keep your identity secret?"

"That should be obvious to a woman of your intelligence, Lady Appleton. I could scarce investigate mine uncle's murder if I was the prime suspect."

"But you were already here when Lord Glenelg arrived."

"Aye."

"Why?"

"That, I fear, must remain confidential."

"Gilbert, please," Catherine whispered. "Give her reason to trust you."

But he remained stubbornly silent.

Vexed, Susanna threw up her hands. "If you are not the killer, who is?" she demanded.

"I wish I knew," Gilbert said. "No one is ever seen near any of the victims beforehand. There are no clues."

"Bodykins," Susanna swore. "It is as if the devil himself swoops down to claim his own."

Immediately, she swore again, this time at a clatter of pottle and trenchers from just outside the partially open door. Whoever had been there had dropped a tray and fled.

"Nan! By nightfall the entire castle will be convinced that if it was not another crazed killer sneaking in from outside to take a life, then it was some fiend, a supernatural being, bent on who knows what foul design."

Gilbert glanced at Catherine and forced a smile. "For once," he said in a bleak voice, "I agree with Lady Appleton."

33

Gilbert felt sorry for Lady Appleton. Neither the coroner nor the justice of the peace would listen to her. Lord Madderly was no help at all. Either he was in deep shock at the murder of his sister so soon after that of his wife, or he was a very clever killer himself. At his insistence on this morning after the crime, the petty constable had taken the local cunning woman, old Mother Coddington, into custody. Just to have someone to blame, as far as Gilbert could see. He'd never heard anyone claim before now that she consorted with devils. On the contrary, folk who thought they'd been bewitched went to her to take off a spell.

"There is no reason for her to kill Beatrice," Lady Appleton protested when the constable informed her of the arrest.

The constable disagreed. He claimed it was well known among the villagers that the old woman thought the Madderlys owed her more than the simple cottage she lived in and a pension.

"For herbal lore? Or something more personal?"

The constable scratched his head, bewildered, and had no answer. Gilbert felt some of his sympathy extend to the fellow. Constables had a thankless job. If they did not make arrests they could be fined for failing to do their duty.

"I mean that Beatrice may have been with child by her lover. Mother Coddington brought herbs to her, possibly to get rid of it. But she was paid for that. Well paid."

Taken aback, the constable gaped at her. The church frowned on the killing of unborn children, though everyone knew it was done. What shocked him to his core was hearing such a charge so plainly put against a noblewoman.

Gilbert wondered if Lady Appleton was right. Had she guessed correctly that Beatrice had a lover? She'd been wrong in her conclusion that he was the noblewoman's secret swain, but there *was* that love bite.

A more serious complication occurred to him then. Was it possible someone had deliberately set out to use this same misconception against him? He knew well enough that if Catherine or anyone else had come to the schoolroom *after* he'd arrived in response to that forged note, he'd have been accused of Beatrice's murder.

"I do make 'a tell th' truth," the constable promised as Gilbert's attention returned to him.

"You would do better to leave that poor old woman alone," Lady Appleton informed him. "If any one person is responsible for all three murders, then that person resides here in Madderly Castle. No outsider could slip in and out without being seen."

Her stand sparked Gilbert's grudging admiration, but he doubted her opinion mattered to anyone in authority. The constable wanted a scapegoat and he was certain he had one in Mother Coddington.

"Talk to Lord Madderly," Gilbert suggested to her as they watched the official scurry away. "He can free the old woman if he chooses to do so."

"Oh, I mean to talk to Lord Madderly. Never fear. He cannot let an innocent suffer to save his family's reputation."

"If you are right about the child, he will doubtless agree with you, for that rumor will do the Madderly name no good."

"Whose child was it?" she demanded.

"If there was a child."

"If there was a child, whose was it?"

"Not mine, Lady Appleton. Of that you may be sure." He sent her a rueful smile. "I have been celibate as a priest since coming here."

"I never trust priests," she declared. Turning her back on him, she swept out of the room.

And she did not trust him, not in matters of murder, and not with her young friend Catherine.

34

need to reassess my suspects," Susanna Appleton told
Magdalen in the evening of the day after Beatrice's death.
"I also need a sounding board, and I no longer have
Catherine, not so long as the list of possible murderers in-
cludes Gilbert Russell." The two women were in the tower
workroom.

"You have a list?" Magdalen wondered why she should be
surprised. Lady Appleton was the most organized person
she'd ever met.

"We start with Lord Madderly," Lady Appleton said.
"Would he commit multiple murders to hide the real one, the
killing of his wife because she deceived him? His grief may
all be an act. His attempts to blame first unknown outsiders
and now Mother Coddington seem ill devised, but were it not
for my presence here, they might succeed."

"He seems unlikely to have killed any of them. Oh,

241

Eleanor, perhaps, in the heat of anger, but not the others."

"You are yourself next on my list, Magdalen."

"You suspect me?" She almost smiled at the absurdity, but it made a kind of sense. Lady Appleton left no stone unturned.

"I did, until I realized that the only guilty secret you were keeping concerned your poems. Before that I reasoned that you might have killed Lord Glenelg, then conspired with your husband to manage Lady Madderly's death when she found proof of your guilt."

"Why would I have killed Lord Glenelg?"

"There are rumors he came here to meet a fellow conspirator in a treasonous plot. You might have been that person."

"Treason?" Appalled by that notion, Magdalen wanted to ask for details, but was given no opportunity.

"Then there is your husband," Lady Appleton said.

"Why would Otto kill anyone?" She started to scratch her arm, then stopped herself, clenching her fists to contain the urge.

"One possible motive occurs to me. What if Lord Glenelg did more than annoy you? What if he seduced you? Or struck you?"

"I doubt Otto would care." Magdalen sighed deeply. "He most certainly would not exert himself to avenge my honor."

"That brings us to Gilbert Russell, Lord Glenelg's nephew and heir."

Nodding, Magdalen applied herself to considering this proposal. She liked Gilbert, but he had behaved badly. "Why did he keep his identity secret?" she wondered aloud.

Just this morning, Lady Appleton had announced it to the

justice of the peace with half the household present. To her chagrin, the justice's reaction had been to bow to Gilbert, assuming that a nobleman could not possibly be guilty of any crime.

"He'd have reason to want his uncle dead," Magdalen continued, "but why kill anyone else? And why stay on here once the deed was done?"

"You make valid points," Lady Appleton conceded, but Magdalen saw she did not cross Gilbert off her list. "What of John Wheelwright? He had words with Lord Glenelg in the library before his murder."

"But what reason would he have to kill? Unless he was this mysterious conspirator."

"That is a possibility I have considered," Lady Appleton assured her. "I wish I had thought to ask about him in Oxford, where he claims to have taken his degree, but I have since written to friends there. I expect a reply daily."

"Lady Appleton," Magdalen began. "This conspiracy. What has treason to do with Lady Madderly's death?"

"It seems certain there is a link between the conspirators, who are producing forgeries as part of their plot, and a counterfeit genealogy Eleanor Madderly foisted on her husband. She was not Sir Humphrey Radcliffe's daughter and I have not been able to discover her real antecedents."

"You could ask Mother Coddington," Magdalen said.

"Surely you do not go along with this absurd idea that *she* killed all three victims?"

"Oh, no. But she must know something about Eleanor's past. Mother Coddington was her old nurse. Eleanor brought her here after she married Lord Madderly and gave her that cottage and paid a boy to help her in her garden, too."

Susanna hid her surprise well, but Magdalen was feeling absurdly pleased to have told her something she did not already know when the workroom door slammed open and Otto barreled into the room. Magdalen bit back a shriek. Otto's face was contorted with a mixture of rage and anguish.

"You killed her, Magdalen!" Otto shouted. "You killed Beatrice."

Astonished, Magdalen could only gape at him. He'd left Madderly Castle on an errand for Lord Madderly shortly before Beatrice's body had been discovered. He'd have heard of her murder on his return, which she calculated could have been no more than an hour earlier, after supper. But somehow he'd already found time to drink himself into a temper. She could smell strong Xeres sack on his breath from halfway across the room.

"Are you mad?" she shouted back. "Why would I kill Beatrice Madderly?"

"You were always jealous." Otto ignored Lady Appleton's presence entirely and advanced on his wife, his knobby fingers curled into fists and raised. "You killed her to get back at me."

Magdalen was too numbed by sudden understanding to feel any fear. It was not Otto's way in any case to use brute force. He wounded her well enough with words or by ignoring her. And it seemed she'd been wrong. Beatrice had not been too proud to lie with the master of horse.

"You betrayed me," Magdalen whispered, revulsion thickening her words. "You betrayed me with *her*."

"She was more woman than you'll ever be! And you killed her!"

He was reaching for Magdalen's throat when Lady Appleton's cold voice stopped him in his tracks. " 'Tis a frequent ploy of guilty men to attempt to shift blame," she said. "But who, I ask you, is more likely to kill a woman than her lover?"

Only then did Otto seem to realize he had a witness. Like a cornered rat, he looked from side to side, seeking an escape route.

"Did *you* kill your mistress, Master Harleigh?" Lady Appleton asked. "You had reason, I suppose, when she told you she'd disposed of your child."

The hectic color in his face intensified. "Witch!"

Lady Appleton blanched but did not back away, nor did she let him stare her down. She seemed to be studying his reaction as calmly as she investigated the properties of a new and interesting herb.

"God's curse on both of you." Otto spat, then shouldered his way out of the room. Neither woman moved until the last echo of his footsteps on the stairs had faded away.

Magdalen sank down on to the nearest stool. Her knees were too weak to hold her upright. "I never guessed," she whispered. "How could I have been so blind?"

Lady Appleton did not answer her. Instead she prepared a posset of soothing chamomile and mandrake seeds. Silently, Magdalen drained the cup.

"You will spend the night with Catherine and me," Lady Appleton told her, "and on the morrow, refreshed and well rested, we three will begin again to search for answers."

35

DUNFALLANDY

Sir Robert Appleton had an uneasy feeling about this meeting. Bad enough they'd had to ride so far north, into the first range of the infamous highlands of Scotland in the biting cold of late January, but added to that was the ignominy of being dependent upon a woman, not only to make arrangements but also to translate.

Annabel shifted restlessly at his side on the rough-hewn bench. Her clansmen, five of them, all great burly fellows, had taken up positions outside the rude hut where they waited for Peadar. There was little danger of being caught unawares by brigands, but neither did Robert feel in control of this mission.

They were all foreign to him here. Peadar. The highlanders. The lowland Scots. And Annabel, too. He'd never known her to take the lead this way, at least not outside of bedsport. But after his return to Edinburgh, she'd seemed to change. He'd merely mentioned needing to find Lord Glenelg's man. The next thing he knew, Annabel had announced they had an appointment in Dunfallandy on St. Margaret's Day.

Peadar appeared at the appointed hour, but he did not seem any more enthusiastic than Robert was. A small, wizened man wrapped in close-woven wool, he ignored Annabel and addressed Robert with a guttural sound that might have been either a greeting or a curse.

Annabel spoke to him in his own heathen tongue, then produced cheese and barley-bree, as if food and drink could make their conversation civilized.

"Ban-Albannach." Peadar's contempt was obvious.

"Meaning?"

Annabel shrugged. "Scotswoman. I do not think Master Peadar approves of me."

"Tell him we already agree on something, but neither of us has a choice."

Peadar chuckled when she translated and asked for a "whang o kebbuck." Annabel passed the cheese. After a few bites, he seemed more inclined to talk, or as he put it, "crack thegither."

Robert asked questions. Annabel translated. Peadar answered, always tersely. Slowly a picture of Lord Glenelg's last days at Madderly Castle emerged. According to Peadar, Glenelg had gone there to meet a confederate, but Peadar claimed he did not know this person's name.

Would he say if he did? Robert wondered. For all he knew, Peadar had been involved in the conspiracy himself.

"Was Lord Glenelg the leader?" he asked.

Peadar replied in the affirmative, leading Robert to hope

that the conspiracy had fallen apart now that Lord Glenelg was dead. Certainly there had been no new reports of forgeries coming out of Gloucestershire. If he could make that seem his doing, Robert thought, he might yet claim a reward. He might even be named to replace Tom Randolph as the English ambassador to Scotland, if he could discredit Randolph's man.

"Ask him whether he thinks Lord Glenelg's heir had aught to do with his death," he ordered Annabel.

The answer that came back confused him. "He says he knows naught of the heir and cares less. The new laird is in Sasunn. England. Born and bred there. A foreigner."

"Tell him the new laird is the same man who discovered Lord Glenelg's body. He was at Madderly pretending to be Lord Madderly's gentleman usher." Sent there, Robert now knew, to spy for Tom Randolph. That fact, however, did not clear him of suspicion in his uncle's murder. And Randolph had been annoyingly closemouthed about Gilbert's precise mission.

For a time, Peadar said nothing. Then he exploded into angry speech. Annabel's eyes grew bright as she listened. "There is your killer, then," she translated, obviously deleting expletives. "Who else would want Lord Glenelg dead?"

"Quite a number of people as I understand it," Robert muttered. "Ask him who succeeds if Gilbert Russell is executed for murder."

But further questions elicited little more information. Robert gathered only that the next in line to inherit Glenelg's title and estates was a good Catholic lad, as the late Lord Glenelg had been. Knowing such a one would be preferred in Dunfallandy over the laird from Sasunn, Robert had to suspect everything Peadar implied about Gilbert Russell, but he decided he'd best report all Peadar had told him in his next dispatch to Queen Elizabeth. Let her determine if the fellow was telling the truth. After all, she was the one who'd set two of her courtiers to competing with one another, giving no hint to either of what she'd instructed the other to do.

36

MADDERLY CASTLE

A good night's sleep seemed to help Magdalen more than it did Susanna. She awoke to a dull ache in her bad leg, the sure harbinger of bad weather. Ignoring the discomfort as best she could, she limped down to the great hall to find Gilbert Russell.

"Where is Mother Coddington being kept?" she asked. If the old woman wasn't held right here at Madderly Castle, Susanna expected her to be in a secure house in nearby Campden.

"She's halfway to the shire town of Gloucester by now," Gilbert told her. "She'll be turned over to the sheriff to hold in his gaol until the next assizes."

"A long wait for an old woman. This miscarriage of justice must be remedied."

"And how do you propose to do that?"

"I will confront Lord Madderly, force him to confess that it was only his desire for petty revenge that made him accuse the old woman."

"Revenge?"

"What else could it be? Anger because she gave her support, years ago, to Eleanor's claim to be related to the earl of Sussex. She was Eleanor's nurse, which means she may well know the identity of our killer, assuming that person is the same one who forged Eleanor's genealogy."

"You believe Lord Madderly accused Mother Coddington of murder out of pique? That seems most shortsighted of him."

"As I will point out to him. He must withdraw the charges he has made and send someone to fetch Mother Coddington back to Madderly Castle, where I can question her. If he does not agree to this, then I shall take it as proof that he is himself the guilty party, and tell him so, too."

"I think," Gilbert said, "that it is time we began to work together."

Susanna gave him a suspicious look. "Why?"

"For greater efficiency?" He gestured for her to precede him out of the great hall and into the parlor behind the dais. It was deserted at this hour of the morning.

Susanna thought it more likely his changed attitude was due to his feelings for Catherine. He'd been giving a good impression of late of a man struck down by cupid's arrow. As a result, she was beginning to reassess her objections to him, always assuming he did not turn out to be their murderer.

"Will you help me persuade Lord Madderly to free the old woman?" she asked him.

"I will. And more. If you first explain what you meant about a forged genealogy."

On the chance he might have unearthed something she had missed, Susanna nodded her agreement, even if she was not yet prepared to trust him completely.

"When Robert and I went to Oxford before Christmas we continued on to Sir Humphrey Radcliffe's home at Elnestow. He was not Eleanor's father. The papers Lord Madderly had to say he was were forged. They may have been counterfeited by the same person Lord Glenelg came here to meet. Your uncle, Gilbert, was involved in treason."

She looked for surprise, even shock. She got a solemn nod.

"I have been aware for some time that he was a traitor. I was sent here to catch him in the act."

"By whom?"

"Certain Scots protestants who contacted me through Thomas Randolph."

"But you are English," she objected.

"Half English. Do you wish to hear my story or not?" At her nod, he told her that the men who'd approached Randolph had been aware of Lord Glenelg's scheme well before Queen Mary's return to Scotland. The conspirators were a radical Catholic group hoping to undermine the protestant alliance between England and Scotland.

A low bench had been drawn up near the fireplace. Susanna sat there to watch Gilbert stir the embers and coax a small flame to life and listen to his account of rival factions in the kingdom to their north. Glad of the fur-lined gown she wore over her kirtle, Susanna tucked her hands into her sleeves for greater warmth.

"You are half English, raised in England," she mused aloud when he stopped speaking. "Where? I know already it was not in Stratford-upon-Avon. We stopped there also on our journey."

"I was born and bred in London."

"And how did you come to the attention of these Scots?"

"They remembered my mother. She is a widow now, and would like to return to the land of her birth."

"So you agreed to spy upon your own uncle."

"Aye. To spy upon him. Not to kill him."

Susanna wanted to believe him, but nothing Gilbert had said removed him from her list of suspects. "Tell me, then, if you do wish to pool our information, all that you know about the murders."

His account took a long time and yielded nothing she had not already suspected, except that he now claimed those nocturnal rides of his had been his means of contacting his confederates from Scotland. He'd met a courier in a tavern in Campden. The rest of his tale served only to confirm what Susanna had already guessed. Gilbert had taken the knife from Lord Glenelg's body long after he'd been stabbed. But had two hands touched the weapon, one to kill and one to conceal it, or had they been one and the same?

"Who do you suspect?" she asked him.

"Lord Madderly," he said promptly. "Lord Glenelg must have learned Eleanor's secret and tried to use the information to convince Lord Madderly to help the conspirators. It follows, then, that he also killed his wife, an act of revenge because he'd learned she'd deceived him."

"Why wait so long after finding out? And Beatrice? What

motive could he have to kill his own sister? Besides, when Robert told Lord Madderly what we'd discovered at Elnestow, Madderly gave every appearance of hearing it for the first time."

Gilbert said nothing, unable to refute her logic.

"Did you suspect Beatrice of the earlier crimes?" Susanna asked.

"Until she was herself killed, yes. That is why I was spending so much time in conversation with her." A wry smile lifted the corners of his mouth.

"Mayhap you were right. Could Lord Madderly have killed her to avenge himself on her for murdering Eleanor?"

"After he learned of his wife's deceit from Sir Robert? I think not."

"Then what if Beatrice and her brother were both in league with Glenelg to forge documents from the beginning?" She frowned. "But then why would Beatrice kill Eleanor?"

"For the same reason I once ascribed to you, Lady Appleton. Jealousy. The desire to take over production of Lady Madderly's great work on herbs."

"I could not have killed Lord Glenelg."

"Lady Madderly might have."

Susanna's head was beginning to ache. "You go as far astray as I have. Who else is left?"

"Magdalen."

"No."

"She has some secret."

"Aye, but not that."

After a moment, he accepted her judgment without explanation. He added wood to the fire, then leaned against the mantel, his gaze fixed on her. "That leaves us with the household officers, none of whom seem likely."

"Steward. Chaplain. Master of horse. Acatar. Schoolmaster. Gentleman usher."

"Back to me. But Lady Appleton, I am innocent."

"Let us talk for a moment about Peadar," she suggested.

At his ease now, as if his conscience troubled him not at all, he answered willingly. "Peadar said he knew me by my likeness to my mother. We came to an agreement while I searched mine uncle's effects after his death. Peadar transferred his loyalty to the new Lord Glenelg and promised not to reveal my identity to anyone until I gave him leave to do so."

"If he recognized you, others might have. By your signet ring, perhaps?"

"I did not wear it after Lord Glenelg arrived."

"And when was it stolen?"

"It has not been. I have it here, if you mean the ring I got from my mother. I have another with my father's crest that I have always used for sealing letters." He reached into a placket and removed a small velvet bag. "Hold out your hand." He tumbled a heavy gold ring into her palm, nearly the twin of the one she had found clutched in Eleanor Madderly's dead hand.

Silently, she produced the signet ring she'd taken from Eleanor's body, studying them side by side. Gilbert's was smaller but the crest was the same.

"That must be mine uncle's ring," Gilbert said. "It must have been taken from his possessions after his death."

"Not from his person?"

"He wore several rings when I knew him, but not that one."

"And it was stolen before you searched his rooms?"

"When else would the killer have been able to obtain it?"

"More to the point, when did the killer learn who you are?" She toyed with the ring, turning it over and over, wishing it could speak. "Did he overhear some conversation between Lord Glenelg and Peadar? Or did Lord Glenelg himself tell someone? And what does Peadar know that he did not tell you?" She looked up sharply. "What did you ask?"

"Every question I could think of." Irritation flashed briefly in those eyes Catherine doted upon.

"Who his master conspired with?"

"Peadar said he did not know."

"And you believed him?"

Gilbert's silence was answer enough. He had been shaken more than he wanted to admit by his uncle's murder and the knowledge that he might be suspected of killing him. He'd missed the opportunity to pressure Glenelg's man about the reason they'd come to Madderly Castle in the first place.

"Why is it so significant that the killer knew who I was?" he asked, swinging one long leg over the bench to sit facing her as he took his ring back.

"Because someone has deliberately tried to cast blame your way, killing two women and planting evidence which points to you. In Beatrice's case, you had a letter. In Eleanor's, this ring was clutched in her hand, as if she'd taken it from her killer."

Gilbert's fists clenched and unclenched. His jaw tightened. But when he spoke, his voice was even, his manner calm. Susanna could not help but admire his self-control.

"So, if he did not have me in mind before I removed the

bye-knife from Glenelg's body, it must have occurred to him then that I'd make a handy scapegoat. But what I do not understand, Lady Appleton, is why you concealed the ring all this while."

She gave him a sharp look. "I do not know. Instinct, I suppose. The certainty that there was something of importance about the ring and that I would be better served if only a few people knew of it."

"What people besides yourself?"

"Catherine, my husband, and Magdalen."

"Suppose Glenelg recognized me when he first arrived here, but for his own reasons gave no sign of it?"

"Go on."

"He might have told someone, someone other than Peadar."

Susanna's eyes narrowed as her suspicion grew that Gilbert had not been completely honest with her. "Are you saying he *did* recognize you."

He had the grace to look sheepish. "Aye. Peadar admitted to me that Lord Glenelg planned to cause trouble for his nephew, but Peadar said he did not realize Glenelg meant me until much later. And of course, Glenelg was killed before he got around to it."

"Well."

"Am I on your list of suspects once again, Lady Appleton?"

"There do seem to be a great many holes in your story."

"Had I known I'd need witnesses to my whereabouts, I assure you I'd have arranged for them."

"And I would then think them knights of the post."

He smiled at that. "Hired perjurers? With what would I have paid them?"

"Promises? Threats?" But in spite of her words, Susanna realized she was once again softening toward this rogue. She also realized that he was right. By working together, they would accomplish far more than if they continued at odds.

As long as he was not the murderer himself.

Later that same day, Susanna was in her bedchamber staring out the window at the road below as Gilbert Russell galloped away. He was going to Gloucester to rescue Mother Coddington from the clutches of the law. With luck he would catch up with her and her armed escort en route and be back in a few days, but in the interim there was naught for Susanna to do but wait.

Time would hang heavy upon her until their return. Magdalen was no help. After his unmasking as Beatrice's lover, Otto had vanished and his abandoned wife was indulging herself in noisy self-pity. In her own way, Susanna supposed, Magdalen had loved her husband and thought him, if not devoted to her, at least faithful.

No doubt Otto had run off into the hills to lick his wounds like the animal he was. Susanna wished she could take this as proof of some greater guilt, but although she could make a case for him losing his temper with Beatrice and strangling her, she did not think him a likely candidate for treason or for the two previous murders.

And yet *someone* had killed three times.

Eleanor's hidden notebook still intrigued and mystified Susanna. She was certain Eleanor had used some sort of code in writing it. The entries were too commonplace. If all she'd intended to do was record the weather and the days she planted certain herbs, then why secret the information away?

Then, too, the notes began after Lord Glenelg's death. There had to be some significance in that.

"Good afternoon, Susanna." Catherine had a cheerful smile on her face as she breezed into the room. In fact, she had the look of a woman who had just been thoroughly kissed in farewell. "How bist?" she added, giggling. "Did you hear? Nan says the ship are down from the hills."

Startled, Susanna stared at Catherine, then looked back at the page she'd been puzzling over. She'd tried reading a message into the words formed by the first letter of each line. She'd read them down each side of the page, and up, and backward, all to no avail. They made no sense in English or in Latin. But in the local dialect . . . could it be that simple?

Susanna scrabbled for paper and quill. For each "he" and "she," she substituted the letter *a*. "You" turned into an *e*. *v* and *f* were transposed, as were *z* and *s*. Dropping the *w* in some words left her with an *o*. Susanna's excitement grew as she translated page after page. There was no mistake. She had found the key.

"What is it?" Catherine asked. "Have you discovered who killed her?"

"That would be too much to ask. But I know more now than I did a short while ago." She studied what she had written. "Eleanor thought she knew who killed Lord Glenelg. She learned Glenelg had been involved with a forger and guessed this forger was the same person who created her false genealogy."

"Someone in this household?"

"It appears so. She writes that it is but a short step from extortion to murder, which I take to mean that this person had already demanded something from her in return for his silence about her background. Money, perhaps. Or a post here at Madderly Castle."

"You cannot still suspect Gilbert!"

"I think him unlikely, but I will discount no one but myself and you, Catherine. Even Lord Madderly must be included, for he could still be the man Glenelg came here to meet. Madderly could have hired the forger, not knowing of the connection to Eleanor. Or he and Eleanor might have been conspiring together, even as far back as the creation of her lineage, if he wanted to give her more standing in the community, for example, through her connection to an earl. Nothing in this notebook contradicts such a notion."

"What else did she write?"

"Eleanor says that she means to meet with the forger, to make sure there is no more trouble. Fool! A name safely recorded here might have saved her life. Instead she confronted this man, threatened him or his employer in some way, and was killed."

"This helps not at all then." Catherine glared at the small leather-bound book.

"It confirms some of what we guessed, a connection between forgery and treason and murder. But why kill Beatrice?"

Had she discovered who killed Eleanor? With all the creeping around she'd done to meet her lover, she might have stumbled upon something incriminating. Was that why she'd been killed? Or had her death had no purpose save to make Gilbert look guilty?

"More questions," Susanna muttered. "Always more questions."

37

The snow began before Gilbert reached Stanton, slowing his progress and making him wonder why he'd agreed to make this trip at all. Only fools, madmen, and robbers stayed on the roads after dark, and dark came early in January. He stopped for the night at Didbrook.

"Snow do balter on th' haarse's veet," the ostler at the inn cheerfully informed him. Gilbert gave the lad a halfpenny to see to the animal's needs and went in search of food and warmth for himself.

All hope of catching up to Mother Coddington short of Gloucester faded as the weather worsened but Gilbert pushed on at dawn in spite of the storm. He traveled by way of Winchcombe and reached Prestbury, on the lower slopes of the Cotswolds escarpment, by the second night of his journey. The land was flat leading there, mostly open fields, and the snow finally stopped. After asking directions from a beggar, Gilbert rode past the neglected park once owned by the bishops of Hereford and came into a tiny market town.

He bespoke a room at the King's Arms Inn, a timber-framed brick building on Deep Street, then asked for news of a party of men guarding an old woman. It was the vicar, one Edmund Lightfoot, who gave him the news that Mother Coddington appeared to be ailing. The riders had not stopped, but pressed on to the southwest along the road to Cheltenham. They were likely in Gloucester by now.

The next morning he set out again, passing through Cheltenham and following the road past Churchdown and Barnwood until at last he came to the city. Here the landscape changed once again. The road was flat, but to the east rose the sharp wall of the Cotswolds and on the west lay the hilly Forest of Dean. Gloucester itself was walled on three sides, with the fourth open to the river. Within he could see the spires of a cathedral and eleven churches, and the ruins of a castle.

In spite of the fact that it now more closely resembled a rock quarry than a fortification, the castle was still used as a prison. The deputy keeper in charge had to keep a constant watch else the prisoners simply stepped over the crumbling walls and walked away. Many were confined in the pit, ceiled at the top by a trapdoor bolted on the upper side, but although felons typically were housed there, women accused of felonies had been given a separate accommodation.

Gilbert found Mother Coddington in an upper chamber, herded together with other unfortunate females in a fetid atmosphere that reminded him of a kidcote. The women were held together by light chains called rings, supposedly less painful and heavy than fetters or shackles, but for a frail old body like Mother Coddington they were torture. Incensed, Gilbert used his boot heel to break them before he went in search of the justice of the peace. On his way out he bribed a guard to bring the old woman food and drink and other amenities.

Booth Hall was the site of Gloucester's quarter sessions and assizes. Even though no courts were in session, Gilbert could smell the frankincense used to disguise foul smells when they were. It reminded him unpleasantly of the time when Eleanor Madderly had lain in state at Madderly Castle.

It took an hour's argument to convince a local justice that Lord Madderly's letter, admitting he had made a mistake in accusing Mother Coddington, was sufficient reason to set her free. Only after Gilbert proffered a bribe did he see the sense in putting his seal on the paperwork to order her release.

Mother Coddington was lying on a proper pallet when he returned to the gaol, but she had rallied not at all. Her eyes were closed, and every breath sounded painful. One of the other prisoners looked up at him and shook her head, as if to say there was little hope. Eleanor Madderly's former nurse-maid was too old, too frail, to withstand the treatment she'd received.

Gilbert bent close, determined to ask his questions, desperate to hear the answers she'd have to struggle to get out. Her imprisonment and the trip overland in harsh weather had sapped her strength and left her with an ominous cough. When she opened those watery blue eyes at last, he realized that they both knew she would not survive the journey back to Madderly Castle.

"Who was she?" he asked her. "Who was Eleanor?"

"Radcliffe," she whispered.

He lifted a wooden goblet to her lips and helped her drink, but the watered-down ale did little to soothe her croak. "What Radcliffe?" he persisted. " 'Tis important. We know already that she was not Sir Humphrey's get."

"Ralph," Mother Coddington gasped. "Ralph Radcliffe the schoolmaster and playmaker."

"Who is he? Does he yet live?"

"Dead these two years past," she managed to whisper before another fit of coughing left her weaker than before.

"She was not a bastard, then?"

"Aye, she was. Ralph married another. Had six children by her, all raised at Hitchen." Each word was wheezed, racking her emaciated body. "No room for Eleanor."

"So that, at least, was true." He suddenly felt sorry for Lady Madderly. She'd risen so far, and fought hard against falling all that way back again. Perhaps that was what had made her so dangerous to the conspirators.

He drew breath, prepared to ask more questions, in particular to demand the name of the man who had forged Eleanor's genealogy. But Mother Coddington would reveal no more secrets. With a little sigh, perhaps of relief, the old woman died in his arms.

38

ow can you do this?" Catherine demanded.

"It is necessary. And what better opportunity than while he is away?"

They were searching Gilbert's room, an invasion of privacy that disturbed Catherine far more than it did Susanna.

"What do you expect to find? You know already that he has Lord Glenelg's bye-knife."

"This, perhaps?"

"What is it?"

"The key Eleanor gave me to her workroom. It has been missing since the day she was killed and her murderer used it to lock the workroom door behind him."

39

Gilbert returned to Madderly Castle on the second day of February. He found Catherine and Susanna in the tower workroom, books and sheets of foolscap surrounding them, inkstains on their fingers, and fatigue making them both short-tempered.

He was not in the best of moods himself. The ride back had been long, cold, and uncomfortable. His horse had thrown a shoe, delaying him an additional day. And now he had to impart the news that Mother Coddington was dead.

It did not surprise him to see renewed suspicion in Susanna Appleton's eyes when he'd completed his report.

"At least we know a little more than we did before." Catherine sent him a sympathetic look as she spoke. "And I can tell you something of the Radcliffes of Hitchen, for that place is in my native Lancashire."

"Is the family connected to the earls of Sussex?" Susanna asked.

"I do not think so. Those at Hitchen were a younger branch of the Ordsall Radcliffes, a large and influential family, but only within Lancashire."

"Lady Madderly would have done better to invent a connection there," Gilbert said. "Not so prominent, but less chance of being found out."

"Not so," Lady Appleton contradicted him. "We have a house in Lancashire. And Sir Robert might have detoured there on his way back to Scotland."

"Have you heard from your good husband?" Gilbert asked her. The last missive she'd had from Appleton had revealed Gilbert's true identity. He was not sure he wanted to know what else the courtier had uncovered in Edinburgh.

"Nothing yet, and if this weather continues, it could be some time before I receive another letter."

"Meanwhile, you are trapped here with a killer."

"Gilbert! You must not say such things."

"Did you think I meant myself, Catherine?" He fingered the little cat she had carved for him as a gift. He wore it attached to his belt for a good luck charm.

"No, of course not." But she blushed prettily.

Clearing her throat, Lady Appleton gave them both a sharp look. "I suppose the very fact that you came back argues in your favor," she told him, "and so does Catherine's continued devotion to you, but there are too many unanswered questions. I like this not."

"I like it no better, Lady Appleton."

"We found the missing key to this workroom while you were gone."

"Where?"

"In your chamber."

He didn't bother to protest the unauthorized search. It was obvious to him that Lady Appleton had not been the first to violate his privacy. "Planted, I assure you."

"Why?"

"For the same reason the signet ring was left with Lady Madderly. For the same reason I was supposed to be found with Beatrice's body. I gave this matter much thought on my journey. If I am found guilty of murder, any murder, then the title and lands of Glenelg descend to a distant cousin. I know little of this man, save that he is a native of Dunfallandy and likely raised a Catholic. With him as laird, the faction involved in this treason can move forward again with Glenelg resources behind them."

"Are you very rich?" Catherine asked.

He had no chance to answer before Lady Appleton posed a question of her own. "If the forger killed Lord Glenelg, why would these people want him to go free?"

"For the greater good? These are fanatics, Lady Appleton. Wedded to treason. Their cause must seem more important than any one man. Whoever this forger is, he is skilled. They need him more than they needed mine uncle. And I, for certes, am expendable." The thought galled him. What did he have to look forward to in Scotland even if he did solve this murder and clear his name? It did not seem likely the people of Dunfallandy would welcome him as their laird.

He cast a longing gaze in Catherine's direction. Any future for them seemed impossible. If he was accused of murder, there would be no hope at all. And if he was not, matters were little better. How could he ask Catherine to marry him and live in Scotland when his future there was so uncertain?

"What you say makes a kind of sense," Lady Appleton said slowly.

He had to think a moment to remember what he had told her. "But who is the forger? And are the forger and the killer the same man?"

"Or woman. I do not rule Magdalen out, even though I am fond of her. Lord Madderly is still a possibility. So is Otto, who has not yet returned but who has been sighted skulking about in the wolds since he ran off."

Gilbert shook his head. He had difficulty imagining tall, gangly Otto Harleigh as the aloof Beatrice's lover, let alone as the mastermind behind all the troubles here.

"I still have questions about Master Wheelwright, too," Lady Appleton told him. "As yet I have received no answer to a letter I sent to Oxford to inquire about him."

"I can reassure you there, Lady Appleton. Wheelwright is in constant correspondence with several men at the university. Why, almost every mail packet contains letters going one direction or the other."

"Have we made any progress?" Catherine asked. She sounded as disconsolate as he felt.

"The herbal proceeds apace." Lady Appleton's lips curved into a small, rueful smile. "Now that there is no one left to argue with me on its organization, it is near completion."

Gilbert glanced down at the cluttered worktable, noting she had been consulting Andrew Boorde's *Brevyary of Helthe* and both the original Latin version and an English translation of Master Vives's famous *The Instruction of a*

Christian Woman. Or, more particularly, its section headed "Medical Knowledge for Women."

"When the herbal is done," he asked, "will you and Catherine leave Madderly Castle?"

"Will I give up before the murderer is caught and punished, do you mean? No."

Catherine nodded vigorously to show her agreement. When her eyes locked with his, Gilbert almost found himself hoping they never solved this crime.

The next few days crept by. At least Catherine had the "great work" to occupy her. It gave her a sense of purpose, Gilbert thought, which he lacked. He spent his time going over the little they knew, but no solution miraculously appeared.

Then the party of strangers rode up to Madderly Castle. Gilbert went out to greet them, introducing himself as Lord Madderly's gentleman usher. He expected their leader, slightly overweight, stern-looking, and wearing a beard in the same style favored by Sir Robert Appleton, to ask to see the baron. Instead the fellow fixed a steely eye on Gilbert himself.

"Gilbert Russell, ninth Lord Glenelg of Dunfallandy," he said in a loud, carrying voice. "I arrest you in the name of the queen. You are charged with the murders of Niall Ferguson, eighth Lord Glenelg, of Eleanor, Lady Madderly, and of Beatrice Madderly."

40

Catherine could not bear the thought of Gilbert, her Gilbert, locked in the castle dungeon. Even though the room was aboveground and he was being well cared for and well fed, she deplored the necessity for keeping him close.

"He is innocent," she insisted.

Walter Pendennis would not listen to her.

"Why are you so convinced of his guilt?" Susanna asked the queen's man.

"You have read your husband's letter for yourself, Lady Appleton," Pendennis said. "The information he learned from Peadar combined with details of this third murder here at Madderly Castle have convinced the queen of Gilbert Russell's guilt."

"Of his guilt? Or of the need to resolve matters quickly and keep scandal at a minimum?"

"What does it matter? The queen has ordered the arrest. I am here to carry out her wishes."

"Then you are a fool, Walter Pendennis."

At his start of surprise, Catherine's interest quickened. There was more going on here than she'd thought. Much more. More than Susanna realized, too.

Walter Pendennis took the set-down most personally.

"There is an obvious explanation for Peadar's claims," Susanna said. "Robert even hints at it in this latest letter. If Peadar is in league with the same group Glenelg was, he'd want to get rid of Gilbert as the new Lord Glenelg. The next heir is a Catholic, is he not? Someone who will support this treasonous cause?"

Catherine's heart soared. Susanna did believe in Gilbert's innocence. And, believing, she would find a way to prove it. Catherine was certain of that.

"It may be as you say," Pendennis conceded, "but no plot in faraway Scotland tells us who murdered two English noblewomen."

"Then we must ourselves complete the task of finding out."

"How?"

"By setting a trap. I will let slip to Nan, my maid, that I know the truth and intend to depart on the morrow for London to lay evidence before the queen. It will not be difficult to make it seem as if I wish to claim all credit for unraveling this mystery for myself. Such gossip will spread like wildfire. I've no doubt the killer will hear of my plans within an hour. I will count on you, Master Pendennis, to order Gilbert set free and give out that a mistake has been made. Affect chagrin. Let it be seen that you think I know the killer's identity but will not confide in you."

"And do you?"

Susanna cast an enigmatic smile his way and continued to lay her plans. "If the killer wishes to silence me, he must act tonight. He will come for me and we will all find out who he is because you and Gilbert will be watching for him. I will bait this trap in the library, I think. There are two ways in, the main entrance and the door behind the arras."

Was Susanna really intending to risk her own life to save Gilbert's? Catherine was filled with trepidation. This did seem the only way to accomplish their purpose. She knew that in her heart. But she feared the danger would be far greater than Susanna admitted.

"I cannot let you do such a thing," Pendennis protested. And again Catherine sensed what he was trying to hide. This man had much more admiration for Susanna Appleton than was proper from one of her husband's close friends.

"You cannot stop me, my dear. You can only aid me. Say that you will do so, for Robert's sake?" She put one hand on his arm and gazed up at him, exerting more feminine charm than Catherine had ever seen from her. Perhaps she did sense Pendennis's regard.

Grudgingly, he agreed and went off to free Gilbert. Catherine was confident the two of them would put their heads together and devise a scheme to protect Susanna.

"Who is it you expect to come?" Catherine asked when the two women were alone.

But Susanna would not say.

At dinner she wore a smug smile as she announced her plans to set out for London on the morrow to purchase books she needed to complete the herbal. If Nan had run true to form, everyone in the great hall believed she had another purpose.

Lord Madderly said nothing. Morose and preoccupied, he concentrated on his food.

Magdalen scratched industriously at her forearm. Otto had been sighted again, much the worse for drink, at a nearby farmstead.

Master Wheelwright stroked Bede's light-colored fur and cleared his throat. "May we bear you company as far as Oxford, Lady Appleton?" he asked. " 'Twas my intention to take Edward and Philip there in a week or two, but with my lord's permission we might go earlier."

"Go," Madderly muttered. "I care not."

But Catherine did. "Why are you taking the boys to Oxford?" she asked when Susanna had nodded her agreement and announced she still had work to finish up in the library before she left.

"You yourself alerted me to their unhealthy interest in witchcraft," Wheelwright said, lowering his voice so only she could hear. They sat with Magdalen, the steward, and the chaplain at a lower table while Lord Madderly, Lady Appleton, Walter Pendennis, and Gilbert shared the dais. "They are not too young to matriculate at the university."

"Ten and seven?" Catherine had never heard of anyone younger than eleven beginning studies at either Oxford or Cambridge.

"They are bright boys. They will do well. And I, of course, will stay to tutor them. Tell me, Mistress Denholm. Do you journey to London also?"

"Yes," Catherine told him, making up her mind to go in that instant. If Susanna's scheme did not work, she might need protection on the road. At the least, Catherine could provide an extra pair of eyes to watch for ambush.

And she could assist in guarding the library, too, she decided. She had just remembered something Susanna had told her Robert had said. There was a third entrance, through Lord Madderly's study. If Madderly was the killer, as Catherine had always suspected, he could slip in and attack Susanna without being seen by either Gilbert or Master Pendennis.

41

As she had planned, Susanna sat alone in Lord Madderly's library pretending to take notes for Lady Madderly's herbal. It was late. Everyone else had gone to bed. Or so they'd claim if a fourth murder victim was found here on the morrow.

The candles above her were sputtering, burned so low they were about to go out. She was getting sleepy, and hoped her guards were faring better, concealed near each of the three entrances to the library.

Bless Catherine, she thought. Susanna herself had completely forgotten about the secret door in Lord Madderly's study. Gilbert had chosen to watch that. One of Pendennis's men was assigned to the main entrance and Pendennis had posted himself at the exit behind the arras. Catherine had been ordered to stay in her bedchamber. Susanna doubted she'd obeyed. She was likely sharing Gilbert's watch.

What else had she forgotten? Susanna wondered. If her scheme did not work, she must find some other means to unmask a killer.

She rose, hoping to keep herself awake by roaming among the book chests and aumbrys. She tucked one hand into the placket in her kirtle, to warm her fingers, and encountered in her pouch the apple Catherine had carved for her.

Slowly she drew it out. Indeed, she had forgotten something. Or rather neglected to draw an obvious conclusion. On some level she had known for weeks that Master Wheelwright must be an expert at carving. If he could teach Catherine to create animals and fruits, then he was certainly capable of carving counterfeit signets. And then there were his letters to Oxford. Gilbert had mentioned how regularly he wrote. It only made sense to think he should have sent word to his confederates in that way. And that Wheelwright had alerted them to the trip before Christmas, too. Likely he'd thought Robert and Susanna were going to Oxford to ask questions about him.

Feeling there was no time to waste, Susanna went to the door behind the arras and told Walter Pendennis what she surmised.

"I will take young Lord Glenelg with me and make an arrest," Pendennis declared when she'd made her case. But he hesitated to leave. "Promise me you will remain here until we have him in custody. I will leave my man at the main entrance."

Susanna found his concern endearing, if unnecessary. If Wheelwright had intended to come, he'd have been here ere now. She was certain of it. "You have my word."

She had materials to put away. She'd keep herself busy.

She might even begin a letter to Robert, telling him of the successful conclusion of their venture. She hoped Master Wheelwright would confess. Or that they would find proof of his guilt among his possessions. She did dislike loose ends and her speculations had not yet yielded a clear reason for Wheelwright to progress from treason to murder.

Lost in speculation, Susanna did not at first notice a sudden draft, not until it was followed by a loss of illumination. From the balcony, someone had created an eddy of air sufficient to extinguish the remaining tapers in the candle beams. Only two faint lights still glowed, the candle on the armariola and the shuttered lantern in a murderer's hand.

Whispered words snaked toward her through the semidarkness. "The time has come to put a stop to your meddling," said the disembodied voice. Wheelwright? She thought so, but she could not be certain. There were still reasons to suspect Lord Madderly. And Gilbert.

Footfalls pinpointed his location on the stairs. He'd come through the hidden door in Lord Madderly's study. His voice confirmed it when he spoke again. "Do not trouble to scream. No one is left to hear you, even if the sound could penetrate the library's heavy doors."

Better to reach one and flee, Susanna thought, whether he spoke the truth or not. She squinted against the darkness, trying to get a good look at her stalker, positive identification, in case he managed to slip out of the clutches of the law when she escaped.

"Why?" she asked. "Why kill Lord Glenelg?"

"I did not care to be threatened." The voice was closer, but still a whisper. With the diminution of light, the speaker was only a dark shape against a greater blackness.

Susanna ducked behind the nearest storage chest. She did not intend to be easy prey. The same darkness that had been meant to frighten her now served as some protection. The room was large and full of shadows. She got down on her hands and knees and crept from hiding place to hiding place, always keeping the bulk of a chest or an aumbry between herself and the killer.

Sensing her movement, for surely he could not see her, he moved to cut off the most likely escape route, the door behind the arras. To go back the other way, toward the main entrance to the library, she would have to move out into the open. Susanna dared not risk it. What remained? The balcony? Had he left the door to the study open?

Her breath came in short gulps as she crept from one shelter to the next, ever vigilant for sounds of pursuit, but the man in the room with her was light on his feet and moved with deadly stealth. Only now and again did an odd scrabbling sound in his wake.

Just as she reached the foot of the balcony stairs, a new light pierced the shadows. But here were no burly rescuers bursting in to save her. Only Catherine stood at the main entrance, a branched candelabra in one hand. Behind her lay the motionless form of the guard Walter had left.

"Get help!" Susanna shouted at her. With a burst of speed, she bolted up the stairs and across the width of the balcony toward the entrance to Lord Madderly's study.

He caught her easily, pulling her back from the open door, but his lantern had fallen on the stairs during his rapid ascent. She still could not see his face.

Strong hands seized her shoulders, forcing her toward the railing at the opposite side of the balcony from the stairs. He seemed intent on throwing her over into the library below. "Let her go!" Catherine shouted.

The scream for help that followed, together with the sound of light, climbing footsteps, startled Susanna's captor just long enough to allow her to break free. She flung herself to one side, toward the heavy aumbry that held Lord Madderly's collection of illuminated Books of Days.

"Go back down." The voice was unrecognizable, a guttural command issued low and loud. He seemed to know that Catherine had not been heard, for he showed no fear of capture.

Susanna prayed her young friend would heed the killer's warning, but she should have known better. With a rustle of fabric and a whiff of violets, Catherine eluded him and joined Susanna behind the aumbry.

That left them only one option. Afraid to speak for fear of warning their enemy, she seized Catherine's hand and pressed it against the back of the heavy piece of furniture. Together they pushed against the solid surface as the threatening footsteps came closer. The aumbry rocked forward a little, but did not seem inclined to do more.

Susanna threw every ounce of strength she possessed against the cabinet. With Catherine's weight added to hers, it at last began to tip.

In the darkness, their pursuer did not realize what was happening until it was too late. There was no time for him to move out of the way, no time for more than a strangled cry to escape him as the heavy oak aumbry bore him to the floor with a resounding crash.

Then there was nothing. No sound. No light. No movement save for the settling of dust.

With trembling fingers, Susanna felt for the candle, steel, and flint she always carried in the pouch hidden in the placket of her kirtle. Fumbling only a bit, she managed to strike a light.

From beneath the aumbry little showed of the man who had killed three times and attempted to kill again. Not enough to tell with certainty who he was.

Not Lord Madderly. She knew that. And unless Otto Harleigh had returned in secret, there seemed only two possibilities—Gilbert Russell or John Wheelwright.

As if to answer her question, the ferret crept out of hiding and began to sniff at the motionless hand showing beneath the aumbry.

"The schoolmaster," Susanna murmured, "as I thought."

Catherine nodded. "I should have realized sooner. Before you were nearly killed."

"My dear girl, you saved my life," Susanna said briskly, "though 'twas passing foolish to rush in as you did." With an effort of will she conquered the shudders racking her body. "Now that we are both safe, you must tell me how you came to the conclusion that Master Wheelwright was guilty of murder."

"Both Master Wheelwright and Lady Madderly came originally from Lancashire," Catherine explained as she gathered Bede into her arms and cuddled the ferret as if it were a child in need of sympathy for the loss of its parent. "Edward noticed the accent ages ago, but I did not realize it was important until tonight."

"A link to the false genealogy," Susanna agreed. "Did you come back to tell me?"

"Yes. Gilbert thought it too dangerous for me to go with

them to make the arrest." She smiled. "I was halfway to our chamber when I decided to join you here instead. I fear I do not take orders well."

The two women found Walter Pendennis and Gilbert just leaving Wheelwright's room.

"The villain you seek is in the library," Susanna told them. "His body lies very near the spot where Lord Glenelg died." Then she told them about the dead guard. Wheelwright had somehow managed to creep up on him and stab him in the back.

The next few minutes were a blur of activity. Lord Madderly was fetched. Messengers were dispatched to the constable, the coroner, and the justice of the peace. Again. Susanna asked Catherine to break the news about their tutor to Lord Madderly's sons, then organized a search of the dead man's possessions. It yielded nothing out of the ordinary.

Finally, Susanna stood back and thought. They had found no papers, no signets, no evidence at all that Wheelwright had been involved in either forgery or treason. "I think we had best question Edward and Philip," she suggested.

"Master Wheelwright kept a book hidden in his desk," Edward revealed when Catherine brought the boys in.

"Where?" Gilbert had already searched it thoroughly. So had Susanna.

Edward pressed a carved rose and stepped back. A panel opened, revealing a notebook similar to those Eleanor Madderly had used.

" 'Tisn't very interesting," Edward explained, drawing it out and giving it to Gilbert. "We looked at it because we thought he'd write about tumbling maids."

Gilbert started to open the book, then stopped and

glanced at Susanna. "Lady Appleton," he said formally, even adding a little bow as he handed it over.

"What is in it?" Catherine asked. "What did he write?"

"It appears to be an account book," Susanna answered. "A record of payments. He names names. The false genealogy for Eleanor is one of the earliest entries. This seems to confirm that he used the threat of revealing the truth about her to persuade her to hire him as the boys' tutor."

He'd seen the advantage to being here at Madderly Castle, where Lord Madderly's collection of letters gave him access to seals he might copy. He'd made quite a business of carving wooden signets and using them to seal documents of his own, documents he had forged in both content and signature.

"This account book seems to indicate he worked alone until recently, making a tidy profit producing passports and bills of exchange." Toward the end of the entries, however, the amounts Wheelwright had been paid increased abruptly. Susanna concluded this was the point at which his fame had spread. When he'd been approached by the conspirators, he'd apparently agreed to work for them because they paid so well. Their "cause" had been of little interest to him.

"Does he list the names of other conspirators?" Gilbert asked impatiently.

"Aye. Two men in Oxford. I warrant you'll find he corresponded with them regularly." She fell silent as she came upon a document tucked into the back of the account book. It was a work of art, and a very dangerous piece of treason, too. "He did fine work," she murmured, handing it to Pendennis.

His face blanched at what he read. "Are there others like this?"

"I do not believe so." She went back to the notebook, which blessedly was not in any kind of code or cipher. "To judge from the dates written here, Wheelwright suspended his forging activities after the first murder. No doubt he was waiting until he'd succeeded in framing you, Gilbert, to resume production."

"Why do you assume that?" Pendennis asked.

"It seems likely Glenelg told Wheelwright that his nephew was here at Madderly Castle. They'd have guessed why. When Wheelwright killed Lord Glenelg, he had a ready-made scapegoat, though when you removed the bye-knife, Gilbert, you thwarted his plan."

"And the signet ring?"

"I imagine he searched Lord Glenelg's possessions after the murder. Perhaps with Peadar's assistance, if your uncle's man was part of the conspiracy. He'd have wanted to make sure there was nothing there indicating he had ties with the murdered man. Perhaps he took that ring thinking he might find a way to use it to implicate you. As he did."

"But why kill Glenelg at all?" Pendennis asked. "He was the source of Wheelwright's income."

"That much Wheelwright did tell me before he tried to kill me," Susanna said. "Glenelg threatened him in some way. I can well believe it. From what I've heard of the man, he lived to make other people's lives difficult."

"And why kill Lady Madderly?" Pendennis persisted. "A quarrel among conspirators makes sense, but not the death of an innocent lady."

"Not so innocent. She had the best of reasons for knowing Wheelwright was both a forger and an extortionist. She must have suspected he'd killed Lord Glenelg and foolishly confronted him. I do not know if he planned to kill her, but he had the ring with him to leave on her body."

Likely Eleanor had tried to order Wheelwright to leave Madderly Castle. Perhaps she had threatened to tell Lord Madderly the truth herself, rather than keep a killer under her roof. Susanna doubted they'd ever know exactly what had led Wheelwright to his second murder.

"I think now that Wheelwright must still have been in the workroom when I returned," Susanna mused aloud. "He waited until I'd gone, then left, taking my key with him. He meant all along to plant that in your chamber, Gilbert, another attempt to make you seem guilty."

"And Beatrice Madderly?" Pendennis asked. "Why kill a third time?"

That was harder to answer. "I believe," Susanna said, "that she was murdered solely to cast suspicion on Gilbert. Wheelwright must have been getting desperate. He knew questions were being asked, but the ring had not come to light and the only thing gossip held Gilbert guilty of was sleeping with Beatrice. Wheelwright took a risk killing her in the schoolroom, but perhaps that was the only place to which he felt he could safely lure both her and Gilbert."

Pendennis shook his head in disbelief. "The man was mad."

"The man was a traitor," Gilbert corrected him. "And I warrant he did not intend to give up such a profitable enterprise simply because one of the conspirators proved difficult. If his correspondence with Oxford was the way he communicated with the others, the fact that it continued means he meant to go on forging documents." He clenched his fists at his sides. "I should have suspected earlier. I was aware of his letters."

"I, too, should have seen the clues," Susanna ruefully admitted. "It all seems so obvious now, though a great deal of what we have concluded is naught but speculation."

"Even so," Catherine said, "we have answered almost every question."

"What remains?" Pendennis wanted to know.

Catherine looked pointedly at Gilbert. When he simply stared back, looking miserable because he knew his future continued to be uncertain, Susanna took the initiative.

"My young friend wishes to marry," she said. "I do not believe she has any objections to living in Scotland afterward."

"Indeed," Catherine agreed, "I would live happily anywhere my husband dwelt."

Pendennis, taking their meaning, seemed shocked by such forwardness. The boys grinned. Susanna felt only relief when she saw the smile blossom on Gilbert Russell's face.

They'd not have an easy time of it, she thought, but at least she now had no doubt in the world that Gilbert and Catherine truly cared for each other. Giving Gilbert a nudge in Catherine's direction, she took Pendennis's arm and steered him from the room.

"Come along, Edward, Philip," she called. Then in a soft murmur meant more for herself than any of the others, she added, "A June wedding, I do think."

42

R obert watched the bride and groom exchange vows with an ill humor he did not trouble to hide. The happiness of others did nothing to dispel his dark mood.

In a few moments, Catherine would become Lady Glenelg. She'd have a title. A Scots title, but still a title.

Susanna had overseen the last of the editing on Lady Madderly's herbal. It was even now at the printer's, about to burst upon an unsuspecting world as the product of female minds.

She was pleased, too, by the addition of a new waiting gentlewoman to the household at Leigh Abbey. Magdalen Harleigh. A woman who had no idea where her husband was. She might be a widow or an abandoned wife and might never know the truth of the matter. Worse, she had joined the ranks of women whose writing had been published. Her poems were being heralded as exquisite bits of whimsy, and were already much quoted at court.

Court!

While he had been stranded in Scotland by heavy snows, Walter Pendennis had presented Queen Elizabeth with the forged document found at Madderly Castle. It would have played a key part in a plot to force Elizabeth to break off relations with the protestant Scots. Because they'd thwarted that scheme, Pendennis was now Sir Walter and Gilbert, after his marriage, would find a welcome at both the English and the Scots courts. His widowed mother would be going to Dunfallandy to pave the way for him to return there later, but the new Lord Glenelg would first pursue a career in diplomacy in Edinburgh—taking Robert's place!

He had done all the preliminary work.

His *wife* had risked her life.

It was not his fault Peadar had lied. Annabel should have been able to tell. There was a lesson he'd learned well: Never trust a woman to translate.

And just where was he to be sent now? He was not welcome in France, not after the warning he'd received more than two years ago. Scotland no longer held prospects for advancement. That left only the Netherlands and Spain.

Spain?

Sir Robert supposed a trip to sunny Spain would be better than cooling his heels at home, or worse, dancing attendance on the queen at court.

Yes. Spain. A country ruled by a king, a man some said should have continued to reign in England after his wife died.

It was not too late for Elizabeth to marry her sister's widower even now. The proper order of the universe could still be restored.

His thoughts were interrupted by Susanna's comments on the future happiness of the bride and groom. He didn't really listen to what she said, just nodded and said, "Yes, my dear."

He'd always been very good at lying.